"You will be my wife... It is written in the heavens."

The Indian's eyes were fixed on Maggie's hair, glowing in the last rays of the dying sun. His hand lifted now to touch it. . . .

"I am Red Eagle." He gestured to the signs painted on his covered chest, pointing things out. "The sun. Coming up. Going down. The birds who hunt. You will be good medicine for me. . . ."

"But—" Maggie sputtered.

He silenced her. "It will be. It is written in the heavens." He motioned toward the still-falling sun. It did seem to be taking its time tonight, almost hesitating in place before making its final journey below the horizon. . . .

He turned to Johnny. "I trade you for this woman. Make good trade, in good faith. Ten horses."

Johnny blanched.

"Twelve horses."

Gathering his courage, Johnny answered, "I would rather not trade her, sir. I am quite accustomed to her, you understand. She is a good cook, a good mother to our children. . . . I cannot accept the offer you make in good faith. Many horses may make a man rich in belongings, but many horses cannot cure the sickness here." Johnny held a clenched fist evocatively over his heart. "It is better to remain poor and keep one's honor with the Great Spirit."

KATHLEEN KARR is the author of several romance novels, including the best-selling *From This Day Forward*, which won the "Gold Medallion" award for romance fiction.

Destiny's Dreamers / Book One

Gone
West

Kathleen Karr

Heartsong Presents

For Larry, who made
the whole journey
with me.

ISBN 1-55748-390-6

GONE WEST

PRINTED IN U.S.A.

July, 1845
Nauvoo, Illinois

"I'm kicking you out until morning. Git!" said the doctor. The man was on the short side, gray-haired and plump, the image of a kindly country doctor in his mussed frock coat and frayed shirt. He didn't seem a bit like a fanatical, self-righteous Mormon as suggested by others.

"Your wife is going to be fine," was added as an afterthought. "She just has to work at the baby in privacy. Come after breakfast and I'll hand her back to you, along with a fine youngster."

Johnny Stuart hesitated in the late afternoon sunlight, running a hand through his curly black hair, feeling the worry pump through his long, lean frame. He badly wanted to stay—to hold Meg's hand, to comfort her in her time of trial. But there was Jamie to look after, and the horse and wagon, too. He finally turned and walked away from the doctor's house, into the sun easing down over the Mississippi.

Nauvoo spread around him, its fine houses leading up to a grand church sitting on the highest point of the city—a golden angel on its steeple, sunstones and moonstones decorating its facade like chubby gargoyles. He didn't take in much of it, though. His heart and mind were back with his laboring wife. What if something were to go wrong? If something happened to her? No. She was strong. It would take

more than the birthing of a first child to stop Margaret McDonald Stuart. She flashed before him—the
flaming red hair, the spirit in her eyes. His wife was
a fighter. She'd be fine. Still. . . .

"Pa?" His six-year-old adopted boy was tugging
at his coat sleeve.

"Yes, son?"

"Ma's going to be all right, isn't she?"

He tried to sound sure, as sure as if it had already
been written in a book. Books were definitive. They
had all the answers. "Yes, and you'll soon have a
little brother or sister."

Jamie took his father's word as gospel. He always
did. "Well then, I'm hungry. Didn't have any dinner
today. And it's past suppertime."

They went to look for supper, wandering along
the street that faced the river. There they found a
little place that seemed to be serving food, and it
wasn't a saloon. Mormons didn't seem to go in for
them, either.

Johnny led the boy in and ordered steaming bowls
of stew and mugs of chilled milk. He was shifting in
his pocket for a few coins in payment when he
noticed something through the window. Jamie was
watching now, too, the ring of milk around his
mouth shaping it into a big "O" of interest and
surprise.

"A mob of men coming, Pa. And they look angry."

Johnny peered more intently through the pane of
glass by their little table. It was a mob. An angry
one. Maybe twenty-five, thirty men, armed with muskets, clubs, and rocks. The men filled the street in front

of them, facing a building opposite with the words TIMES AND SEASONS neatly painted on a sign. It didn't appear to be a healthy situation by any stretch of the imagination.

Johnny's first reaction was to throw the coins on the table and grab the boy by the hand. Get him away from this street. Fast. He'd been told Nauvoo wasn't a good place to be stopping, but when Meg went into labor on their wagon, Johnny wasn't fussy. He'd heard about this Mormon city in their travels. It was in the middle of some kind of war with its neighbors. Something to do with the killing of the Mormons' "Prophet" and leader, Joseph Smith, back last summer.

The doctor had seemed all right, though. And the rest of the city was quiet and peaceful, not to mention clean. It had to be the cleanest town Johnny had ever seen—no pigs and garbage in the streets, and the streets themselves laid out in cobbles—not mud—straight as a razor, at right angles to each other. It would've been a good place to sell books if he hadn't had Meg and the baby worrying him.

"Pa, I don't think I want to go out there. They're shouting now."

"Hush, Jamie. We'll sneak behind them. They've other matters on their minds besides us."

They were outside the little eating place now, edging into the shadows around the corner of the building, the river spreading out behind them, beneath the bluff. It was a good drop down, maybe fifty feet or more. Johnny pushed Jamie closer to the wooden slats of the wall so there'd be no danger of his falling. He made a quick survey around them. They couldn't slip behind the building. It was sitting on the very brink of the cliff. Maybe they'd best try to make themselves invisible right here until the ruckus passed.

"Down behind that bush, Jamie, and leave room for me!"

The shouting increased while they made themselves as small and inconspicuous as possible. Figures were jostling each other, fists and clubs raised in anger. The fighting had spread over the whole street.

Johnny put an arm around the boy and hugged him close, feeling his heartbeat speed. Words whose meaning Johnny didn't understand flew past his ears. Then a rock, thrown askew, grazed his head. Johnny pushed Jamie's head lower and felt for his own. His hand came away wet with blood. He glanced up in time to dodge another missile, feeling as besieged as a medieval fortress. He had to remind himself that this was Illinois in 1845, not something he'd read in a book about the exploits of King Arthur.

Crashing glass brought him back to reality. That and the men storming the shop across the way. Before Johnny could piece together what was happening, the mob was out again, hauling a heavy piece of equipment. The last rays of the setting sun glinted on the object, twinkling from a little brass finial atop it.

"It can't be," Johnny whispered.

"What can't be?"

"*Ssh*. Keep your head *down*. It is. It's a Ramage press. They've broken into a newspaper office!" Eyes wide, oblivious to the dark stain of blood creeping down his cheek, Johnny watched the heavy wood and iron press being hauled across the street toward them.

Johnny shrank closer into the shadows behind the bush, gripping Jamie in a bid for total silence. Those men couldn't be doing what it looked like they were doing.

They were.

They were going to toss the press into the river. A press like that was worth upwards of seven hundred dollars. He knew. He'd priced them out. A press like that was the answer to a man's dreams. His dreams. Dreams of heading farther west. West with his books, and the type for the press he'd already purchased. He'd been scrimping for a year to buy a Ramage press to go along with that type and knew he wouldn't have the price scraped together for another ten. Not with his family to feed, and a new baby to look after.

With grunts and groans, the heavy mass of finely tooled iron was heaved over the bluff.

Slursh.

It was swallowed by the accepting Mississippi.

Johnny waited for rough cheers to die down, waited for the mob to disperse. It didn't. Instead, his ears caught a familiar crinkling sound, and his nose the smell of smoke. They were torching the newspaper building! The smoke thickened around them and Johnny tried to protect the boy from it. Only when the human sounds had ceased did he dare to pull himself from hiding, to move closer to the edge of the drop.

Through the smoke over the river, he spied concentric circles vibrating around a few bubbly belches of air. They hadn't heaved the press too far out. That was good. He marked the spot in his mind—there, with the big boulder nearest it. He already knew what he had to do. Would Dickens, his horse, be strong enough to help? Would Jamie?

Johnny waved smoke from his eyes and swiped at the blood on his face, managing only to spread it over firm cheekbones and along a square-cut chin. He tasted it and grinned. Like a conquering warrior, like one of his Highland ancestors, he wanted to let out a shattering cry of victory.

Instead, he closed his eyes and prayed for guidance. A weight lifted off his shoulders to disappear into the smoke and water. God had truly brought him to this spot for a reason. The *Times and Seasons* office was still smoldering. The newspaper was as good as dead. And Johnny Stuart had the identical salvage rights of any man picking up debris from a sunken steamboat. He opened his eyes with a final prayer that total darkness would quickly fall, bringing the anonymity of night. He gathered Jamie to him in a hug.

With a press like that, his waiting would be over. His family could make for Oregon when the last snows melted in the spring. Johnny leaned over the bluff a final time to watch the river's currents wash out all traces of the press. It was safely hidden beneath the waters. In the morning he'd have his wife, a new baby, and a future.

one

"I've made a list of traveling supplies we'll be needing, Meg." Johnny raised his head from the scrawled sheet before him at the table.

Maggie smiled as she rocked peacefully in her chair, baby Charlotte nodding in her lap. Johnny alone called her Meg. It was an endearment between them since they'd first set eyes on each other ten years back.

"One hundred fifty pounds of flour," he enumerated. "Fifty pounds of bacon, a keg of prunes, ten pounds of lye soap, a rifle and powder—" He stopped with a worried frown. "That's just for starters, and doesn't take into account a wagon and oxen."

"We made it to Independence before the worst of winter set in, Johnny. The Lord is still looking after us. We'll manage somehow."

Johnny glanced around the one-room log cabin they'd just rented for the season on the edge of town. It looked bare with only the board table and benches for decoration, and a big bed, with Jamie already asleep on a little trundle bed pulled out from beneath.

"It's going to be cold, love. We'll need cords of wood for the fireplace, and a cradle for Charlie—"

"Stop fussing, Johnny. Charlotte can sleep between us for a while yet. It will keep her warmer. When I get our pots and dishes spread around, this place will look as close to a home as we've ever had."

Johnny pulled his elbows from the table and got up to throw a log on the fire. He stood for a moment in its glow, shoving wild curls from his forehead. "And there'll be books to order from Cincinnati. I'll have to send a list by steamboat. I never expected to sell as many that last hundred miles—"

Maggie laughed. "I think the baby helped—her cooing and grabbing at your stock like she did every time you opened the side of the book wagon in front of a farmer! Of course you'll need more books, Johnny. Imagine going west without books!"

Johnny pulled the hand from his curls and banged it into his other fist. "I'll have to find a job! There's money enough for restocking, and maybe even the new wagon and animals, but for the rest. . . ."

Maggie bent to kiss Charlotte's silken red head. "Stop fretting and come to bed, Johnny. This is only our first day on the edge of civilization."

That it was truly the edge of civilization was borne home upon the Stuart family as they made time to explore the town. It seemed like one huge wagon-building establishment. Oxen fattened on grass along the rims of the settlement, and exotic people filled its streets. There were scruffy wilderness men aplenty, but it was not they who caught an Easterner's eye.

"Ma! Pa! Look!"

"What is it, Jamie?"

Jamie pointed. "A real, live Indian! With a blanket

and feathers and everything! Walking nice as you please down the street!"

Maggie turned to observe the proud nomadic face with its sun-darkened skin. Remembering herself, she gently took Jamie's pointing hand in hers. "It's not polite to stare or point just because someone's a little different from us, son."

"I'll say he's different!"

After that, it became easier. Braves and squaws and papooses were all over the place once the noticing began. The tribes camped outside of Independence, surviving by trading animals with the westering emigrants. There were Foxes, with shaved heads and painted faces, and Shawanoes, and Delawares. But most of the Indians were of the Kansas tribe. And it was Kansas children that Jamie began bringing home.

It was well into November when Jamie flung open the wooden cabin door, letting in gusts of Missouri winter. Maggie looked up from the cornbread she was pulling from the reflector oven before the fire. His cheeks were rosy, his young body strong. And he was almost twice as tall as when she'd found him more than two years ago—abandoned and half-starved, fighting off street pigs in the winter snow of Cincinnati. She shook away that painful memory.

"You're late for your morning lessons, young man. And for heaven's sake, shut that door—" She stopped. Jamie wasn't alone.

"I brought some new friends home, Ma. Didn't think you'd mind." He turned to beckon forward two figures behind him. They came slowly. By the time Jamie finally had the door shut, Maggie had dropped the cornbread on the table and was pulling her shawl more tightly around her shoulders and giving the baby worried glances, thinking about chills. But Charlotte slept on in the new crib Johnny had bartered for her.

"Ma?"

"Yes?" Her eyes rose from the cradle.

"This here is Straight Arrow and Running Bear."

"Oh. My."

"They're of the Kansas tribe, and they're gonna teach me how to use a bow and arrow."

The two small boys were almost cowering against the cabin walls. They wore greasy deerskin tunics and trousers, and looked cold and hungry.

"Well. It seems as if all three of you could do with some hot broth and a taste of my fresh batch of cornbread." Maggie smiled and cut into the steaming bread.

In a few minutes the boys were dripping butter from their chins, all squatting on the floor, since Jamie's friends seemed uncomfortable with the table and benches.

That was the beginning. After that, Straight Arrow and Running Bear knocked politely on the cabin door each morning—just in time for breakfast. Johnny got used to moving over a few places as the Indians got used to the table. Then Johnny would throw on his coat and head out to the job he'd found as a printer's apprentice for the town's only paper.

He'd pause at the door to give Maggie a kiss, and

smile on his enlarged family. "Have fun with all of God's children today, Meg love."

"I will, Johnny."

The lessons would start. Maggie carried on with Jamie's education as if nothing were different. The newcomers listened with wide eyes, slowly becoming brave enough to ask questions of their own. After a few days, Maggie had no choice but to give them their own class on the alphabet, since Jamie had been reading already for two of his six years.

Sometimes Charlotte would sleep through the lessons, and sometimes she would wake to kick in Maggie's arms and reach for Straight Arrow, whom she particularly liked. He would giggle and let her pull at his dark fingers and poke at his eyes. After the lessons were finished for the morning, Jamie would run off to study the mysteries of the bow and arrow and the cabin would become quiet again.

Well into December, a knock came on the door when least expected, after the lessons were finished and the quiet had set in. Maggie put down her sewing and opened the latch. It had begun snowing again. A blast of fine powder struck her as she stared at the figure so patiently waiting. It was swathed in blankets already inundated with snow. The face peeping out of the wrappings was young, pretty, and Indian.

Maggie recalled the courtesies. "Come in. Please. Come out of the cold."

The woman hesitated, but entered. She stood shyly by the fire, thawing, before she finally turned to speak. "You good woman. Teach Indian boys white man's words."

Maggie smiled. This could only be—

"Straight Arrow and Running Bear my sons. Is good they learn. I come with thanks." She burrowed out of her blankets and presented two furry lumps. Maggie accepted them gravely.

"Rabbit. Good food." The Indian woman's eyes were slowly taking in the cabin. They stopped at the cradle, suddenly bright.

"Baby!"

In a moment she was kneeling next to Charlotte, cooing softly. Charlotte opened her eyes and smiled. "Strong baby." The red hair was touched wonderingly. Then she was on her feet, walking to the two rabbits Maggie had set on the table.

"Pelts. For girl child. Keep cold away from her."

Maggie fondled the soft fur. "How? How to cure skins?" She spoke slowly, hoping the woman would understand. She did.

"My white name Flower Blossom. I teach, as you teach my sons."

Maggie poured Flower Blossom a cup of hot coffee. "That would be marvelous!"

Flower Blossom appeared the next day, directly after lessons. Maggie fervently hoped she hadn't been hovering outside in the snow, waiting. She feared the woman had. Maggie offered coffee and set freshly baked bread on the table while Flower Blossom removed her blankets and opened a small cloth filled with tools.

"Rabbit?"

Maggie presented the skins and had her first lesson in scraping and cleaning. It was the beginning of a friendship.

Flower Blossom came each day, earlier and earlier, until she was sitting in on some of the lessons. Her English began to come more readily, although she never could get closer to "Maggie" than "Ma-gee."

Johnny had purchased his westering rifle and went off practicing with it when work was slow. Fresh meat began to fill the Stuart table, and Maggie and Flower Blossom had more skins to practice upon.

The winter days went faster with Flower Blossom's company as the two women traded recipes and skills. Moccasins were constructed for everyday comfort, and snowshoes for severe winter weather.

Other information was traded, too. Maggie learned that Flower Blossom's family was nearly destitute. They had lost their ancestral lands and were caught between two worlds, struggling to survive with honor. It was a new concept for Maggie, and she, in turn, struggled to grasp it.

The white neighbors had not gone long in noticing this interchange. One evening just before Christmas, a delegation banged on the door after the children had fallen asleep. Johnny was cleaning his musket and set it on the table with a questioning look at his wife as he crossed the few yards to the entrance. Four men barged in, blowing frost and snow into the cozy room.

"Evening, gentlemen. To what do we owe this honor?"

Maggie was already up from her chair, reaching for the coffeepot on its tripod over the fire. "It's a cold night. May we warm you?"

"Thanks, but no." The leader's words were curtly spoken. Then he remembered to remove his hat. "I'm Phil Walters, and these here are some of your other neighbors hereabout."

Johnny nodded. "We've passed. I'm afraid we've been too busy to be as neighborly as we'd like—"

"Too busy with them heathens, is what!" growled Walters. "It's what we've come about. Ain't Christian to be openin' your door to all them Injuns. Up to now we've kept 'em on the edge of town where they belong. You people keep lettin' 'em in, next thing you know, they'll be beggin' at all the cabins!"

Johnny stood by the table, fingering his musket. "Our friends have not been begging. Our door is open to any of God's people who seek our help or friendship." His eyes met Walters's directly. "That, sir, is Christian."

Maggie stood rooted by the fire, still holding the hot coffeepot. "I keep a little school here of a morning. If you've children of that age, I'd be delighted to have them join us—"

Walters swung his attention to Maggie. "Ain't no child of mine studyin' with no heathen spawn. Keep 'em in their place is what we need to do!"

Maggie's cheeks flamed as red as her hair. "And where exactly is their place, pray tell? We've stolen their lands. We kill their game. The least we can give them in return is something to fill that gap. Is respect so costly?"

"Maggie—"

But Maggie would not be stopped. "I've learned more in the past month from my Indian friends than I've learned from the *civilized* in years. And I intend to keep learning anything that may help my own family to survive once we head west!"

Walters ignored the spate of vehemence to grasp at that last word. "So you're headin' west with the spring, are you?" He clapped his hat back onto his head. "As there's no talkin' sense into you, it'll be good riddance to troublemakers, then."

The big man shoved the others, silent throughout his tirade, into the dark, and the heavy door slammed. Johnny followed them to check the latch.

He turned around slowly. "I think *I* could use a cup of that coffee, Meg. And where did I set my volume of St. Augustine? I could also do with some righteous pagan baiting about now."

Christmas passed quietly and snugly with the entire Stuart family tucked into the big bed after Maggie's Christmas dinner. Johnny had brought the Bible in with them, and Jamie was curled into his shoulder on one side, Maggie on the other, with Charlotte in her arms. Every quilt they owned was piled high, keeping them snug against the wintery chill of the cabin, while the soft halo of a lantern spread over them.

Johnny read aloud the early chapters from Matthew and Luke, stopping to let Jamie take over in the shepherd and angel parts: " 'And, lo, the angel of the Lord came upon them, and the glory of the Lord shone round about them. . . .' "

"That's always been one of my favorite parts, Pa." Jamie sighed peacefully as he snuggled closer. "Feels kind of like us right here. With the peace and good will and baby Jesus arriving, just like our baby."

Maggie swiped at her eyes and swallowed a snuffle of happiness. The snow lay heavy outside.

It was Johnny who suggested that Flower Blossom's family be invited for a New Year's celebration. Maggie wasn't sure what would happen, but she asked anyway. Johnny also invited a few of the bachelor men who hung around the printing office and who'd been handy with advice on the coming journey.

The men started arriving after dark—newly scrubbed and in clean shirts—bringing such presents as a slab of bacon, a few potatoes, or fiddles to play. The fourth and last, a huge, full-bearded old man, brought a handmade whistle for Jamie and a jaw-harp for his own use.

Then Flower Blossom's family arrived. Maggie almost quailed at the first sight of her husband, Black Raven. He came, indeed, in glory. His head was freshly shaven and painted red, his one tuft of remaining hair dangling feathers and rattlesnake tails. There was bright glass in his ears and a collar of bear claws around his neck. Flower Blossom and the two boys, proud of his elegance, respectfully brought up his rear. Everyone else faded into awed insignificance.

Black Raven's face was fierce, but his arms were full of a deer haunch. Before too long, Charlotte was lodged in his lap, batting at his bear claw necklace. And Maggie was chuckling to herself. The ferocious brave loved babies!

The evening passed with joy, grace, and music.

Spring came at last, and with it, days spent in the fields around Independence, Charlotte strapped, Indian-fashion, to Maggie's back. Flower Blossom and the boys were usually in attendance, everyone hunting for the green sprouts of edible roots.

Flower Blossom most often found a new variety. Eyes bright, it would be flourished in an arc of thanks over the awakening prairie. "The Great Spirit puts good things on this earth, Ma-gee. We must never starve reading His signs."

Maggie was beginning to understand. "I think our God is the same, Flower Blossom. We just give Him different names."

There was comfort in this shared understanding, as there was comfort in learning the Indian ways of making pemmican for traveling food. Maggie was willing to learn any new ways that would keep her family from starving on the great journey drawing nearer each day.

While Maggie was studying with Flower Blossom, Johnny was finishing the last chores necessary for the trip. He'd earned enough for supplies and left his job for the final work of waterproofing wagons and organizing and reorganizing the contents that must see them safely across two thousand miles. He drew steadily more excited as the leaving approached, chafing for the road, chafing for new adventure.

Maggie studied him with love and hope, but also with a touch of exasperation. Johnny. He'd always been a dreamer, his head either in the clouds or in a book. Would this trip work the wanderlust out of his soul at last? Others readying to leave Independence spoke of the journey as their "Manifest Destiny"—spreading out America to where it belonged. Many of the white-tops even had that phrase painted on their sides; others, the slogan "54' 40 or Fight!" Some ignored the politics completely, and only wanted fresh new lands to farm.

But Johnny was doing it for the pleasure of the trip itself. It was that pure and simple true. Not that he'd ever admit as much. His precious Ramage press and the opportunity it gave him for work when they reached Oregon was just an excuse, the final excuse to justify the two thousand miles.

"Meg," he'd say, "Meg, there are new lands out there, places I've read about, dreamed about. I can't rest till I've seen them."

Her Johnny would probably never rest. She might have a real house for a while once they made it to the Oregon country—a snug little cabin like this one they were fixing to leave—but could it ever be permanent? Would he search for other horizons, farther north? Surely he couldn't go farther west. Farther west from Oregon meant only the vast watery oceans, and he wasn't a sailor. Johnny liked land beneath his feet, as long as it wasn't his own.

She'd married a gypsy. But what a gypsy! Lean and muscled, with that constant light dancing in his eyes, and a sharp mind and loving heart.

When the time came for leaving with the wagon train Johnny had signed them on, it was still hard. Maggie had spent the final night in their little cabin, sleepless, praying for her family long since left behind in Ohio. Praying for friends made along the way. Praying for the Indians she'd come to love. But mostly she prayed for the deliverance of her own small family.

She joined the train in the morning with dry eyes, but knew her heart wasn't leaping like her Johnny's was. Still, it mattered not where he led her. She would follow him to the ends of the earth, then up to heaven when the world got too small.

two

A hungry wail jarred Maggie's ears. She gave a shout, but continued walking next to the oxen, skirts tucked up against the pernicious mud that caked her boots and legs beyond. Several days out from Independence on the Oregon Trail, the mud caked everything.

"Jam-ie!"

The boy came running back from ahead. He was the only one the mud never seemed to slow.

"Yes, Ma?"

"See to the team for a little, son. I've got to feed Charlotte."

"Sure thing, Ma."

He snatched the rawhide whip from her hand eagerly, cracking it a few times in glee. Maggie had to smile. It was almost longer than he was.

Still smiling, she adjusted the straps of the sling holding baby Charlotte to her back. Waiting another moment next to the slowly revolving wheels to get her timing right, Maggie finally sprang up to the wagon seat protruding from the little caravan the oxen were pulling, and gratefully seated herself. It had been a trying morning already, and the excuse of resting while feeding her baby was welcome.

Carefully maneuvering the baby forward, she let the little one nurse, keeping a good grip on the babe to keep her from tumbling out of her arms.

"Jamie?"

"Yes, Ma?"

"How's your father doing up ahead with his wagon?"

"He says his new boots are starting to break in fine, but Brandy's giving him some grief. Keeps wanting to stop and feed."

She watched the boy prod the animals before them. Next to snails, oxen must be the slowest creatures on God's earth. But they were steady—unlike flighty mules some on the train had chosen—and they were strong. They'd kept the wagons from miring too often in potholes hub-deep from unusually heavy spring rains.

Maggie gazed down at her daughter's fire-red curls and the little fists contentedly kneading her. In between concentrating on her meal, Charlotte enjoyed the animals' slow jogging, the chance to stare bright-eyed at the new sights constantly moving past them.

It was Maggie who missed the forceful trotting of Dickens and Miss Sally, the two cart horses who had brought the family down the Missouri to their wintering place in Independence. The horses were having a rest now. They trailed on bridles behind the covered wagon in front of Maggie's caravan, occasionally trotting around and up front on their long leads to check on Johnny's progress with his oxen.

Johnny's white-top was carrying the heavy portable printing press he'd salvaged from the river in Nauvoo as well as his type, so he had three yoke of oxen. Maggie's wagon was a little cabin on wheels and the family's usual home. It held the books, not to mention sundry other personal possessions, and was led by two yoke of oxen.

The other emigrants on the train had thought the young family demented to attempt to haul two wagons across the trail, with only a woman—a nursing one at that—responsible for half the burden.

Johnny had merely pointed to the sign painted in red on the side of the caravan: JOHN AND MARGARET STUART, BOOKSELLERS.

"We are a team, my wife and I. We've worked together with our books, and we'll work together with our westering." The elected captain of the train, Joshua Chandler, was still doubtful, so Johnny had added the clincher. "You and the others travel with seeds and plows, ready to work the new land. We are tillers of the mind. Are we to leave our tools behind?"

Back in Independence, Johnny had nudged grudging approval from Chandler to join the train of thirty other wagons. Now they were part of a hundred-member family.

Maggie shifted on the seat, leaning gratefully into the stuffed deerskin cushion Johnny had made for her back in Independence. It was one of Black Raven's skins, and it had been her final curing project with Flower Blossom.

If they'd chosen to travel with mules, she could have been sitting the whole time, leading with reins, enjoying this gift from her Indian friends to comfort and ease her. She sighed and shifted the baby to a more comfortable position. She would just have to get used to the idea of walking, regardless of the weather, most of the two thousand miles across the wilderness to get to their promised land.

Acclimation had already begun during the first two days. The last of the winter rains had continued, the heavens seemingly uninterested in the miseries its onslaught brought upon the little band below. Johnny had erected an umbrella above the heads of Maggie and her papoose, keeping at least the baby dry, although they must have made a rare sight, indeed. So the coming of the sun's rays this morning had been a blessing.

Charlotte's suckling ceased. The babe had a replete smile on her face and in her jay-blue eyes. Those eyes. They were the color of her mother's, but they danced like her father's. Maggie bent her head to kiss the eyelids and the soft skin of her cheek, such a delicate porcelain. Maggie adored her child more each day.

"Please, Lord," she whispered, "let this little one survive the trip. Let her survive all the ailments of childhood. She will make an extraordinary woman. She has spirit, like her father."

The pace of the wagon changed from a slow bump and crawl to a squeaking halt. Maggie looked up. Noon already? Easing herself and the baby to the muddy ground, she arranged her dress more modestly, then went around to the back of the wagon and climbed the two steps to open the narrow door. Inside the tiny cabin, Maggie placed the sleeping child into the hammock Johnny had made for her, suspended from the roof between the bunks and the windows. It was netted all around, and the babe could sleep peacefully without danger of falling, and without buzzing flies or gnats to disturb her.

Outside again, Maggie's eyes searched for her husband. He must be letting the oxen out to pasture. She did so look forward to the sight of him, a little touch or kiss before starting on the meal. One look somehow made everything all right, and gave her the strength for her next job.

Her ears pricked up. The strains of "Summer is icumin in" were being whistled with abandon. A long shadow fell from behind the wagon, and suddenly Johnny Stuart was following it.

"And how is my lady holding up this fine spring day?"

He doffed his cap and made a courtly bow before Maggie. When his eyes were lifted again to hers, she saw the laughter in them.

Maggie touched his face, already roughened by the weather of the trail. "I missed you."

"And what of me? I miss sitting on the wagon next to you, too, like the old days."

"We've both a lot of missing to go, then, Johnny Stuart." Maggie smiled. "We've hardly left Independence behind."

Johnny kissed her forehead sweetly and was moving again, shoving the old felt hat back atop his black curls. He was incapable of stillness. There was something in him always ready to burst out—a song, an idea, a poem.

"Where are the children, and where's the food? I'm that hungry I could eat an ox, particularly one Brandy. That laggard put me through my paces this morning."

"Charlotte's tucked away asleep, and Jamie could

be anywhere." Maggie was stooping to arrange a few stones for a makeshift hearth. "And you never used to think about food, Johnny."

"I never used to have to deal with six lumbering beasts hour after hour since daybreak, either."

Her eyes reached up for his again. "We're not too far out to turn around, Johnny. There are still miles of roads we've never traveled back home."

"And miss all this?" He gestured at the neighboring women fuming over squalling children and wet tinder, at the muddy ruts of the trail behind them. "Never!" And with an off-key "Loud sing! Cuckoo!" Johnny disappeared after firewood.

Maggie was still chuckling when another male voice caused her to look up from the hearthstones.

"Charley giving you a break, is she?"

Stretching her back from her labors, Maggie welcomed Irish Hardisty, one of her neighbors from the wagon behind. "That she is." She smiled softly.

"It's going to be mighty hard for this man to wait long enough for that young lady to grow up. She'll be a dazzler, she will, the toast of the Oregon country."

This time Maggie laughed. "You seem to have a gifted eye for the ladies, Irish, but you'll be a grandfather by the time Charlotte is of suitable age."

"Not this boy. I'm saving myself."

"Highly unlikely," Maggie replied to his back as he wandered off to inspect the crop of promising young ladies engaged in the trip.

Maggie was dragging a heavy iron skillet out of her wagon when Irish's sister Gwen strolled up.

"Afternoon, Maggie."

"Afternoon, Gwen. Off to collect fuel for your fire?"

Gwen leaned against the brightly colored flowers painted on the side of the book wagon. She slowly let out a sigh and pulled back several strands of blond hair that had fallen from her bun to curl around her ears. "It seems such a waste of energy to hunt for brush on this sodden, treeless plain." A gesture encompassed the almost flat prairie spreading out on all sides of them, its grasses just sprouting several inches of green. "I mean, thirty or so wagons, thirty or so fires. Mightn't it make a lot more sense to consolidate the effort?"

Maggie hid a grin. How had this woman chosen to go west? "This is only the third day out, Gwen. But go ahead, haul over some bacon. My skillet's big enough for all of us."

Gwen brightened visibly. "It's not that I mean to take advantage, Maggie—"

"I know."

"It's just that Irish, bless him, disappears as soon as the oxen are let off to graze. I can't do much complaining to him, either. He's my little brother, not my husband. I can't allow him any excuse to ship me back east. Give me a piece of cloth and I could sew up a storm, but I haven't quite gotten this campfire business organized in my mind yet."

"I've had plenty of practice, Gwen. Lend me a hand and I'll have you building a proper fire in no time."

"God bless you, Maggie Stuart." Gwen sighed

with relief. "I couldn't think who else to ask. The other women give me strange looks, if they deign to look upon me at all. Although what is so strange about a spinster traveling with her younger brother, I have not yet conceived."

Maggie gave Gwen another glance, from the rich, sun-golden hair right down to the rest of her neighbor's perfect hourglass figure. "Not strange at all, if you've looked at yourself recently, then looked upon most of the others. You're comely, Gwen, with none of the hard look of having borne six or eight youngsters and put up with a stubborn man in the bargain."

"It was by choice, I assure you. Although I confess I get all shaky every time I see you nurse your Charlotte. Love lights up the two of you, from inside out—like a madonna and child. Most of the other women, they seem to spend their days yelling at their offspring. Then when they're good and wound up, they let into their men."

"Maybe they didn't come by choice, Gwen. It's a hard thing to do, having to follow your man into the wilderness. It's a lot easier if you've done it by free will and love, as I have."

"Well, if I had a man like your Johnny, I'd follow him clear to China. He's just like out of those romances—*Ivanhoe,* or something. You expect him to be wearing shining armor instead of mud-spattered trousers!"

Maggie laid down the skillet and reached into her skirt pocket for her little match safe. Johnny's performance had not gone unnoticed. She decided to ignore the comment, but her heart skipped a beat at a sudden vision of Johnny dressed for a tournament, her scarf gracing his lance. "Then again, maybe some of the women are a little jealous of you, Gwen."

"Me?" Gwen was shocked. "I've got nothing. I've left the rock and I'm heading for the hard place. Irish is my only family, and he was so addled by the thought of going west that I couldn't talk him out of it. My only choice was to go along with him, try to keep an eye on him, and maybe help him. He's probably older than your Johnny—he's a full twenty-four years—but he's taking his own good time growing into responsibility."

"It will come eventually, Gwen. Don't worry over it. Every man has his own time." Maggie picked up the skillet again. "We'd better get some food onto a fire before the captain calls time to yoke up again."

Gwen tested a smile. "I'll bring the coffeepot, and some brush I spotted a little way back. No guarantees on how dry it will be, though!"

They were wiping up the last bacon grease from their tin plates with the flour pancakes Maggie had made. Irish put down his plate first and reached into his pocket for a cigar, bending to start it smoothly from a smoldering stick from the fire.

"First thing I intend doing when we get settled in Oregon is find me a nice, rich, clay deposit. Then I can set up my wheel and make some real pots and plates. It's uncivilized to have to eat from metal. Leaves a tinny taste in your mouth." He nodded toward Maggie. "No offense to your cooking meant, not at all."

Irish spread his compact body out on the damp grass, tipped his slouch hat over thick, wavy, chestnut hair and dark eyes, and pulled at the cheroot.

"How can he make plates with a wheel, Ma?"

"It's a different kind of wheel from the ones that pull our wagons, Jamie. Irish is a potter by trade."

"Oh." The boy cogitated on the new information only a moment, then, "May I go and play with some children?"

"Whom did you have in mind?"

"The Kreller girls up toward the front of the train. They're fun, 'specially Matty. I promised to show her my bow and arrows from Straight Arrow and Running Bear. I might even let her try it out. She's my age and can do almost anything I can."

"Only almost?"

"Well, she *is* a girl, Ma!"

"And what about me, young man?"

"You *can* do anything, but mothers are different."

Maggie shot a glance at Johnny, who was biting back laughter.

"Go ahead, son, but head back as soon as you see the camp shifting. We may need you."

"Thanks, Pa!"

"Johnny—"

"He'll learn exactly what girls can do soon enough, Meg. Let him feel superior for at least another year!" Amidst laughter, Johnny eased his much longer frame onto the ground in imitation of Irish.

"The timing of this trip is good." Irish blew out a smoke ring thoughtfully. "If we arrive in October, like everyone expects, there'll be the whole winter to fuss with a proper kiln before I have to worry about getting some planting done."

"Think you can make a business out of making pottery?"

Irish tapped at his ash. "Not right off. I'll make some for my own use and pleasure at first. In another few years, when more folks follow us out, I figure there'll be a need."

"It should be the same with the books," Johnny thought aloud. "But if I can't find enough interest, I'll just drum some up."

"How you planning on doing that?"

"There must be upwards of five thousand Americans in the Willamette Valley and spread out beyond, and if they're not inclined to become educated, I'll just teach the Indians to read."

Gwen, following the conversation as she and Maggie cleaned up after the meal, looked horrified. "You'd teach the Indians?"

"Why not? They've minds and souls the same as we."

"But, but—"

"But what? They're heathens? Let me tell you about a few members of the Kansas tribe we knew back in Independence—"

Just then, however, the call to move floated back to them. Groaning, the two men got up to yoke their teams. Also on schedule, Maggie heard a cry of protest from Charlotte in the cabin. It was time to face the rest of the day.

three

Spirits were high in the prairie camp that night. The long, cold winter was over, and solid weeks of rains seemed finished, too. The prairie hay was greening fast. They'd made twelve miles on the trail. There were reasons for optimism.

The Stuart family lazed under a full moon, Charlotte crawling around a blanket, eager to get the exercise she'd been denied all day. Johnny and Maggie watched her with pride while Jamie practiced jumps from the wagon wheels to the soft grass below.

"Doesn't that boy ever tire?" Johnny asked. "He's already put in twice the amount of exercise we have today running between the wagons."

"He's young and growing." Maggie was tucked snugly next to Johnny's body, his arm comfortably around her shoulder. "In a few minutes he'll just drop in his tracks and sleep till morning."

Johnny glanced up at the sky. "I'm tired enough for that myself. But with a soft breeze and such a moon, somehow I can't set my mind to sleep." He stretched a little. "Jamie!"

"Yes, Pa?"

"Think you can locate the instruments in the wagon?"

Jamie's face lit up with pleasure. "Yes, sir!"

In a moment he returned, laden, to hand a concertina to his father, and a banjo to his mother.

He kept the recorder for himself.

"With all the excitement, I near forgot about the music, Pa. What shall we start with, the one about the pioneers coming to Ohio Territory?"

Maggie smiled as she pulled herself from her husband's half embrace. "That sounds perfect."

Soon they started in, Maggie's lovely voice singing out clear and strong:

> *Rise you up my dearest dear, and present to me your hand, and we'll all run away to some far and distant land.*

At the end of the first verse, the Stuarts were pleasantly surprised to find new voices, particularly the strong tenor of Irish Hardisty, join in on "And we'll ramble in the canebrake, and shoot the buffalo."

When the song was completed, they found they'd drawn a crowd around them, most of the faces new ones, all of them making cries for another song.

"What shall it be, then?" Johnny spoke up cheerfully.

A surprising request came from a big, broad man standing shyly at the edge of the crowd. " 'Home, Sweet Home,' please."

"Come on, you're never homesick already, are you?" joshed someone else.

Johnny quickly intervened. "It's a fine American song, and we'll do it on the understanding that it be dedicated to our new homes in Oregon." And nodding to Maggie, he started in.

By the end of the song, the crowd was silent.

It was Irish who saved a few potential tears from being shed. "Know the one about the cork leg, Johnny?"

Johnny grinned knowingly. "You bet I do," and launched into a rousing version of the gentleman who had quaffed one too many during an evening's entertainment.

The audience was growing larger now, and all joined in with "He clung to a lamppost to stay his pace, But the leg wouldn't stay, but kept on the chase."

All were laughing good-naturedly at the end, enjoying their new camaraderie when a tall, distinguished man shoved through the group. He stood before Johnny and Maggie glowering, moonbeams outlining the stark nose, the gray at his temples, the unhealthy glint in his eyes.

"Know you not that tomorrow is the Sabbath? Would you insult the Lord with such drivel?"

"I don't believe I've made your acquaintance, sir," offered Johnny, concertina poised on his lap.

"I am the Reverend Josiah Winslow, embarked with my family for the Whitman Mission in the country of the heathen."

"Thought the Whitmans were out in Oregon," piped up a bystander.

Winslow whipped around. "I carry my mission to bring the Word of the Lord to those poor demented souls less fortunate than ourselves, while there still be time to save them, but it would appear that my services are wanting in this very train as well."

"Where are your wife and children, Reverend?"

asked Maggie with complete innocence. "I'm sure they'd like a little joyful music, too. Even on the eve of the Sabbath, I know the Lord wouldn't begrudge us a bit of merriment after a hard day's labor."

He stared down at her. "My family, thank you, is sitting by our campfire, studying their Scripture—" his head slowly made a circumference of those around him—"as all of you should be doing. Know you not that besides the consideration of the Sabbath Eve, it be unhealthy to make such a row out here?"

"Bosh! Ain't a soul aside from us for miles around!" threw in someone.

"I beg to differ with you, sir," Winslow countered darkly. "There could be Indians sneaking around, and maybe even—" his voice lowered—"maybe even *Mormons!*"

His words were received with blank stares.

It was the big man who'd requested "Home, Sweet Home" who spoke up slowly and with consideration. "Mormons be considerable north of us, Reverend. Maybe a hundred, hundred-fifty miles or more to Iowa. 'Sides, from what I last heard, they got their own troubles to contend with. I can't picture 'em sneakin' around the prairie at night spyin' on a friendly train of emigrants. Ain't like any of us is from Illinois and got a bone to pick with 'em."

There were a few "Hear, Hears!" before the preacher chose to answer. "The Saints do their own bonepicking, I assure you. They'll be short on provisions, with tens of thousands of them barely across the river from Nauvoo, sitting there in hunger these past two months. They'll be sending out parties to plunder in the unholy names of their prophets and their god." He glanced around the darkness. "Just mark my words, all of you. If you won't honor the Lord, at least consider your own earthly possessions!"

Johnny looked as if he didn't care for the feet beginning to shuffle uncomfortably around him. Fear—particularly unfounded fear—was not a useful emotion with which to begin a two-thousand-mile pilgrimage.

"I'm sure we'll take all that under advisement, Reverend, as soon as our musical soiree is finished. But we've really only just begun. Right, folks?" Johnny grinned mischievously at the group highlighted by the campfires surrounding them. "In fact, some of our new friends were about to haul out their own pieces and join in." His gaze caught that of the shy giant who'd spoken up in defense of the Mormons. "You there, sir. You look like a man with music hiding in your bones. Have you nothing to contribute to our group?"

The big man shifted his weight from one foot to the other. "Sam Thayer, I be. And I ain't exactly inspired with it, but I do have me a harmonica."

"Haul it out, Sam, and drag it over here with your body." Johnny turned to the others. "What do you say? The trip will be long. Best to start now in organizing a little entertainment of an evening."

There were several prodding elbows, more embarrassed grins, and in a few minutes a fiddle, a guitar, a bugle, and a washtub had been added to the proceedings. The Reverend Josiah Winslow, pained, took his leave with small grace.

Maggie alone watched his departure. Johnny's response had been good for the general morale of the camp. But she didn't care for the disposition of this Winslow. She recognized the type. The Reverend Winslow was a hard man, like her own father. There'd been no music or singing in her own childhood, either. But although stern to a fault, James McDonald had also been fair, and increasingly open to new thoughts as Maggie had grown. Winslow, on the other hand, appeared completely single-minded. He could prove to be a formidable enemy. She pitied the Indians he'd come to save, and wondered what had transpired between Winslow and the Mormons to elicit such obvious hatred.

Then she forgot about the man. Charlotte was asleep in her skirts and Jamie was nodding off against her shoulder. Maggie joined in on another song.

four

Later in the week, at evening, the rains came again in a show of might and fury. The dinner fires were extinguished, leaving only the fire in the sky to light up the darkened camp.

Maggie raced, sopping, into the caravan, Johnny just behind. They dripped on the clutter together.

"Maybe we should have left the children out," Johnny joked. "They could stand a bath, too."

"Really, Pa? May I go stand out in the storm?"

"No!" Maggie glared, at wit's end after the day on the trail. Her vehemence shocked Jamie into silence, and set Charlotte into howls in her hammock. "Listen to me! I'm beginning to sound just like the Jarboe and Simpson women!"

"We're all hungry and tired, love," tried Johnny in a soothing voice. "Why don't I fire up the stove for you?"

Maggie glanced at the little potbellied Franklin stove. "I'm afraid of burning us and the caravan down. It's just too tight in here, Johnny! It was so much simpler before—"

"Come on, Jamie. Up on the top bunk with me." Her husband tried another tack. "Hand me Charlotte to entertain, Meg. Then you can shove her hammock out of the way and at least try to get another dinner organized."

Maggie managed a thin smile as things were rearranged around her. Why was she being so ill-tempered?

Her mother *had* warned her on her wedding day that there would be times like this.

She found a piece of hardened crust for Charlotte to teethe on, then, on second thought, found another for Jamie. "It's the last of the real bread from Independence. Savor it."

The last of the bread, the last of civilization. Maggie stubbed her toes on stacks of grain bags lining most of the walking space before she was able to let down the little table from its traveling spot on the wall between the two windows.

"We should have brought chickens, Johnny. I could have made a cage for the caravan. We could have had fresh eggs."

"There wouldn't have been room for the extra grain, Meg. And you're the expert on farmstock, but it occurs to me that they wouldn't have done much laying, anyway. They'd be too unsettled by the ride."

Maggie was kneeling by the stove, stuffing it with wood she'd been hoping to save for future emergencies. "In that case we could have *eaten* them. It seems like a year already since we've had fresh meat."

She felt in her skirt folds for the hidden pocket, her fingers finding the match safe. "If I can get this going, it'll have to be johnnycakes tonight."

Her breath held until a flame took hold on the grass tinder she'd pushed between the sticks of wood. On her feet again, she found a bowl and mixed cornmeal and water with the sureness of long practice, dreaming all the time of roast chicken, with gravy drippings, and maybe a side dish of mashed potatoes and fresh greens.

The cakes were in the pan, sizzling pleasantly in a little bacon grease, and the tiny, overstuffed cabin was beginning to dry out from the damp, beginning to feel cozy again. Johnny was entertaining the children with a spirited rendition of "Turkey in the Straw," and Maggie had almost worked herself out of her ill humor.

Then the knock came, between the onslaughts of nature.

"It's the door, Ma. Shall I get it?" Jamie's legs were already slipping down the sides of the bunk.

"Stay put, for mercy's sake. I'll only trip over you."

Maggie wiped her floury hands on her skirt and moved the few yards to the door. She opened it a crack. The weather blew it wide, and the soft lamplight of the cabin revealed a dumpling shape concealed in a ground cloth.

Maggie started. "Come out of the weather, if you can manage it."

A grunt came and the wagon swayed. A hand reached out to slam the door, and the covering was pulled off to reveal a fleshy, gray-haired little woman. She stood dripping, blinking through fogged spectacles.

Maggie handed her a clean rag. "What brings you out in this weather, Mrs. Richman?"

"Many kindly thanks." She patted Maggie's arm and nodded a hello to Johnny on his perch. "Might as well call me Grandma, like most folks do.

'Eudora' never suited me much, and 'Mrs. Richman' is a mite highfalutin' for a neighbor come to beg your mercies." She caught a drip edging down her nose with the cloth.

"Truly amazin' weather, ain't it? As if hard rain weren't enough, the Lord's gotta throw in some hail as well. Don't like to complain, but the timin' could be better."

She stopped a moment to take in the pocket-sized cabin and collect her thoughts. "I was castin' about for a live fire and saw the smoke from your wagon by the lightnin'. Got me a grandson just slithered outen the wagon as the commotion in the sky was startin' up. Landed bad on his arm, he did, and the bone broke, clear through the skin." She glanced up at Jamie peering down at her. "Not much older'n your boy up there, Jubal is. Might've seen the two of 'em chasin' around with that Kreller girl. Got him splinted up, best I could, but he's painin' bad, with a fever startin' in and the cold he picked up last few days not aidin' none, neither." She paused. "Thought a hot poultice might help."

Jamie's eyes had widened during her recital. "Is Jube going to be all right?"

"Won't be havin' no jumpin' contests with you for a while, iffen that's what you mean, boy. But he should heal by and by. Trussed up lots of broken bones in my sixty-five years, I have, childern an' livestock alike. Mostly they healed up fine."

Maggie pulled a coffeepot from its hook on the wall and began to fill it with water from the barrel crammed between flour sacks on the floor. "Let's start him off with hot tea. I've some mint that will calm him. Then we can make a poultice of mustard and angelica. Angelica is excellent for soothing inflammations."

"Bless you, dearie. I've brought some mustards, but can't say I've ever tried angelica." Grandma pulled a parcel from under her shawl and presented it to Maggie. Her mission accomplished, she squinted at the little stove while trying to rub the last rain-splotches from her eyeglasses. "But you haven't finished feedin' your family yet!"

Maggie expertly scooped the cakes onto plates, poured a little honey atop them, and handed them up to Johnny. "This will hold my men. I'll send Johnny over with the medicines later. Where are you camped?"

"Just to the north of you, dearie. Three wagons up." Grandma Richman pulled the ground sheet over her head again. "Crowded as 'tis, wisht we had this snug cabin tonight. The weather comes into them prairie schooners somethin' fierce, even with blankets pulled over the openin's. Guess oiled linen'll get you only so far in a mean storm like this 'un. And I thought the rains had finally stopped."

Johnny stared at his empty plate. "The rains will stop soon enough and we'll be praying for them once more. You'd better set out your barrels for filling."

"Tosh. Be happy to see the end of the rain and the sniffles, I will. Well, I'd best be getting back to the youngsters. Cold, wet, and hungry as they are they'll give young Jubal no ground, even in his condition. And their father ain't got the sense I bore him with, neither. Can't control them nohow." She sighed and reached for the door. "Pity his wife died over the winter. And me the only thing keepin' them all going. At my age, too!"

The door slammed behind her and Maggie shook her head. "This train is becoming more like a small town every day—making up for all that solitude I grew up with back on the farm. Hand me that bunch of dried mint hanging right above your head, will you? Next to the marigold and mallow. We've got to help fix up young Jubal. It could have been our Jamie."

Jubal was still in pain the next morning when Maggie checked on him, his injured arm swollen to almost twice its normal size. Maggie felt his brow, and, concerned, lifted her hand away from its heat. His eyes were dull and wide with it. She gave his grandmother a questioning look.

"Freshened up the poultice with the breakfast this mornin', Maggie, and give him a good dose of laudanum, too. Don't know how much else kin be done."

The opiate would account for the dazed expression. Maggie didn't hold with giving it to children—or anyone else, for that matter. "It will be very uncomfortable for him to be jouncing along in the wagon bed all day," she said.

"I know, dearie, but there don't seem to be no other choice."

Maggie thought of Charlotte, and her gently-swaying hammock. "Couldn't we fashion a pallet for Jubal, something like my baby's hammock? A little rope, a few blankets—"

"Hal!" Grandma's yell stopped her before she'd finished. "Hal! Get in here to help fix up a travelin' bed for your poor boy!"

At her call, Hal Richman appeared, a thin, balding, weak-looking man. Maggie wondered briefly how he'd ever had the energy to father so many children. His head dripped water from the rains into the wagon opening. He took one look at his aggressive mother, another at the ailing son, surrounded by a bevy of younger children, scuffling with each other, swinging from the rims of the roof, crawling over a monumentally heavy, ornate bureau.

Shaking his head, he reached unerringly for a jug tucked into the nearest corner. He paused to orient the jug appropriately in the triangle of his left arm, elevate his elbow to the proper height, and take a long swallow.

Grandma bristled. "That demon rum ain't gonna make your problems disappear, son, just blur 'em a little. Now Maggie here come up with a good idea, and we need you seein' steady to put it to use. Tuck that jug away now!"

Hal Richman took another nip, then plugged the jug with its cork. "I be with ye, even though inside the wagon is women's work. But make it quick. Train's fixin' to move on."

Grandma Richman had more to contend with than Maggie had known. Why was Hal Richman bothering with the journey? A man like this could find defeat anywhere. Oregon would not be covered with six-foot-high clover, or have game and fish for the plucking. It was just another new place at the end of the line, a new place that needed clear heads and hard work.

Maggie squared her shoulders. "We need two good lengths of rope, Mr. Richman, and a spare piece of canvas large enough to set your son Jubal on."

He grunted and began his search.

Just past the Little Vermillion Creek crossing, Maggie's oxen blundered into a huge mudhole she'd missed. The book caravan lurched to a halt, and Maggie could almost hear the mud greedily swallowing the front hubs. The sudden silence also allowed her to hear ravenous yells from the baby inside.

A moment later, Jamie was poking his head around the corner of the wagon. "Charlotte's hungry, Ma, and I've memorized three poems from *McGuffey's*, like you asked, plus read most of the stories. I don't care if it is raining again. I got to get out!" He stopped as he noticed his mother's face. "We bogged down?"

Maggie stood studying the reddish-brown slush oozing past the upper spokes of the front wheels. "Run for your father. I don't think I can handle this one. But cover your head first!"

Too late. He was already sprinting into the rain. With a shrug of her shoulders, Maggie waited for Johnny.

When he came, he took one look at her predicament and sent her to deal with the baby.

She'd finished feeding Charlotte and even tucked her back up in her hammock, and still the wagon hadn't moved. What was holding them up? Maybe the wheels were in worse shape than she thought.

"Guess I'll have to unyoke my oxen and bring them back to help haul," Johnny told her when she rejoined him outside. "We've already been passed up by just about the whole train."

Just then a final wagon ponderously caught up with them, hesitated, and stopped.

Sam Thayer appeared through the downpour. "Trouble?"

Johnny brightened. "Usually comes swifter than the things we desire. Can't get loose of the muck. I was just going to fetch my team and haul them over."

"Let me get my extra pair. They're fresher."

"Much obliged, Sam."

Maggie stayed to watch the new team hooked up, to hear the unexpected words coming from the lips of both men as they lunged with the animals. Even Johnny's vocabulary had found new directions in which to expand. She shook her head and honed in on a patch of wild onions.

The last of the hoarded wood was sacrificed to get the potbellied stove fired again that night. It was still raining hard, and if they didn't get dried out now, the Stuart family would be sick soon, like the others. Maggie was not about to let that happen. She pitied every woman on the train without a stove.

Each would be struggling over faltering fires, or just giving up and serving another cold meal.

Maggie got soup going, rich with several pounds of the wild onions she'd gathered. With the broth simmering at last, she turned to Johnny. "I'm going to take the umbrella and check on Jubal. Do you think we could cram Sam Thayer in here if I offered him some soup? It must be hard for him to have to do for himself without a woman. And he did help us this afternoon."

Johnny lit up. "Did you see him just lift the whole wheel towards the end? The man has no idea of his strength. He saved me hours."

"Then it's all right." Maggie smiled. "Jamie, would you like a walk? Pick a handful of apricots and prunes for Jubal. It might help to cheer him."

Jamie tripped over himself and most of their belongings in his enthusiasm. He'd been too long cooped up. "Can I quote some of my poems on the way, Ma?"

"Surely. Come now, before Charlotte wakes and looks for me."

Outside the wagon, Jamie raised his face to the downpour, glorying in it. "One of my poems was about worse weather than this, Ma:

> *It snows! cries the Widow,*
> *'O God!' and her sighs*
> *Have stifled the voice of her prayer . . .*

Maggie cast a sharp glance in his direction. "Are you sure that was in *McGuffey's*, Jamie? And get your head under this umbrella. Now!"

"Sure was, Ma." He lingered outside her shelter long enough to catch a few drops of the rain on his tongue. "Horrifying it was, too, with ten feet of snow pilin' up around the widow's house, and no food to be had. But the Lord sent neighbors to check on her before she had to eat her cat—"

"Jamie!" Maggie was still rooted in the downpour outside their book wagon. "*McGuffey's* never suggested—"

"Nope. But it made sense to me, even though it *was* a mighty skinny cat. Think we'll ever see that much snow, Ma? I mean, if it were just a little bit colder right now, this rain could make ten feet of snow easy, couldn't it?"

Where did boys find their imaginations? "Your bedtime prayers tonight will include a special message to the Lord that we never see such snows, Jamie. At least not until we're safely in Oregon."

"It was only an interesting idea, Ma—"

Maggie was beginning to get very wet. She remembered her errand. "Come along, Jamie. We'll have to figure out which wagon is Mr. Thayer's."

They found Sam Thayer's wagon by dint of its silence. Maggie poked her head in and saw him disconsolately throwing a slab of raw bacon onto a piece of very dry bread.

"Evening, Sam."

He jumped in surprise.

"Could you do with some hot soup for supper?"

His sodden hat was tipped at her, and a grin spread from ear to ear on his homely face. It made him almost handsome, even though his nose had been broken once or twice along the way. " 'Twould be a rare pleasure, ma'am."

"Come by our wagon in about an hour then. The broth will thicken while we visit the sick child at the Richmans'."

Maggie let the canvas flap close on him, almost catching Jamie's curious nose.

"Know why he's so strong, Ma?"

Maggie pulled Jamie closer under the umbrella. "Why, Jamie?"

"He used to be a blacksmith. He can fix anything that moves—wagons and horseshoes alike. He's just like Longfellow's hero:*

> *Under the spreading chestnut tree*
> *The village smithy stands;*
> *The smith a mighty man is he*
> *With large and sinewy hands.*
> *And the muscles of his brawny arms*
> *Are strong as iron bands.*

"You *have* been busy today, Jamie."

"Oh, I memorized lots more."

"Save a few to surprise me with later, son. I do believe my cup overfloweth at the moment."

The Richmans' wagon was easier to find in the sodden gloom. War whoops definitely marked its territory.

Maggie closed in and raised her voice.

---

*From "The Village Blacksmith" (1842).

"Grandma? It's Maggie Stuart."

The flap was raised. "Come in, and welcome, iffen you can stand it. I think Jubal's goin' to make it. The fever broke a while back, praise the Lord."

"Amen!" Maggie let Jamie hoist himself up, then followed. She sidled past the invalid's elevated legs and scrunched up to his head. His eyes were almost animated again. The swelling was down on his arm, too, and he was accepting Jamie's gift with subdued enthusiasm.

"Bet that's the last time you're gonna jump from the wagon," Jamie was saying.

"Not on your life! I'll just be more carefullike next time, is all. Everythin' woulda been all right iffen that big ol' clap of thunder hadn't skittered me. Messed up my timin', it did."

Maggie smiled at the braggadocio. If Jubal was feeling well enough to boast, he'd be all right. She felt his forehead anyway. Still damp and sweaty. He'd be needing some of her hot soup, too. "Come now, Jamie. There are enough youngsters around here already. You can visit again at breakfast time."

She finally had to haul Jamie out and shove him under the umbrella. Then he remembered more poems and recited all the way back.

Sam Thayer was already in the little cabin, cuddling a fascinated Charlotte. There was a bemused expression on his face as she tugged at his thick, bristly, brown mustache and pinched his lopsided nose.

Reasonable father material, thought Maggie to herself. She closed the umbrella and stepped over his legs to check on the cauldron of soup. She had a ladle up to her mouth, tasting, when a tentative tap sounded on the door. Maggie glanced up at Johnny on the upper bunk. What now?

Johnny didn't wait to consider, just belted out a cheerful "Come in!"

Gwen Hardisty entered, tears in her eyes. "Maggie, I'm at my wit's end! I've done everything you taught me, but I just can't keep the fire going in this rain, and Irish is in a black mood from the wet and no hot food, and—" She tripped over Sam Thayer's legs and finally noticed him. "Oh," she said in a small voice, "didn't know you had company."

Sam pulled his mustache out of Charlotte's grasp and nodded, stiffening his back a little.

Maggie checked her pot of soup once more, mentally calculating how far it could be stretched. She turned to a bag by her feet and threw in several handfuls of rice. "Go back for your spoons, bowls, and your brother, Gwen. If you don't mind standing up, I've enough soup here to warm up an army."

The tears stopped. "You're a saint, Maggie Stuart!"

"No," Maggie retorted good-naturedly, "I've just got the only decent fire in camp tonight. But I'm on the last of my firewood, so tomorrow night we'll all be in the same boat, or maybe swimming, from the looks of things."

Gwen raced out as Johnny's eyes met Maggie's. She knew the expression. The "Here she goes collecting more orphans again" look. She grinned at him suddenly. It was true. Her only weakness, and nothing could be done about it. That's how they'd adopted Jamie, after all, and Flower Blossom and her brood. Now here they were with a new set.

Maggie tasted the soup and added a pinch of salt and another of pepper. Come to think on it, there could hardly be a better way to spend a wet night on the prairie—with the sole exception of some complete privacy with Johnny. And that was far from forthcoming.

They were crammed in tighter than the books on the wagon shelves outside, and the soup pot was scraped clean. Jamie had fallen asleep on the top bunk, Charlotte snuggled safely between his body and the wall. Maggie and Gwen sat on the bottom bunk, the men slouching comfortably on grain sacks in front of the women. Irish was sucking on an unlit cheroot, and they were all speculating on their futures.

"I had a word with Josh Chandler this afternoon at the crossing," Irish commented. "He's worried about Pawnee country coming up. Seemed even more concerned about the Mormons, though."

"Does he really expect Brigham Young to sweep down across the prairies and wipe us all out, or worse yet, force polygamy upon us?" Johnny seemed amused at the idea.

"What's *polygamy*?" asked Gwen.

"That's when, that's when—" for once Johnny seemed at a loss for words.

"It means a man can take as many wives as he

wishes, Gwen," Maggie filled in for her husband.

Gwen looked shocked. "Oooh. Is that what that 'Celestial Marriage' business is that the Reverend Winslow's been going on about?"

"They also call it the 'Doctrine of Spiritual Wives'," continued Johnny, more at ease now that Maggie had bridged the awkward moment. They were among a group of adults, after all, even if Gwen weren't a married lady. "There was a wonderful joke going around Independence about it over the winter. It seems that shortly after Joseph Smith came up with this particular revelation, a Gentile lady had the nerve to ask his first and number one wife where the Saints found this doctrine. With eyes blazing, Smith's wife answered, 'Straight from hell, Madam!' "

Chuckles rose from all save Gwen. "The man deserved to be shot!"

Johnny was serious again. "Not necessarily, Gwen. It turned him into a martyr. Worse still, it took the reins of power from a sly, but inefficient man and turned them over to Brigham Young, who's apparently becoming a real leader. From what I've heard, he's transformed Smith's militia and is honing it into an efficient group of killers. They call themselves Danites, and sometimes Destroying Angels—"

Johnny stopped when he saw the frightened look on Gwen's face. He'd gone too far. "But their ways needn't concern us," he added hurriedly. "They're struggling to the north of us, without even proper wagons for shelter. They've no cause or reason to know of our existence—" He halted again. Unless, of course, someone had gotten wind of that Ramage press. He'd not really taken serious precautions to hide their leaving Nauvoo—

No. He shook his head almost perceptibly. That was long ago and far away. It had been fair game. And the Saints had the survival of their people to busy them now. "They've much more serious things on their minds," he repeated aloud for the benefit of everyone, including himself.

"Seems to me you take the Mormon threat too calmly, Stuart, especially after what you've just said."

"They only crossed the Mississippi in February, Irish. Thousands of them. Last we heard in Independence, they were still bogged down at Council Bluffs in Iowa Territory. They've got their own troubles finding a place to take them. They won't have any energy left for marauding."

"That Reverend Winslow sure thinks different on the subject," opined Sam.

"It appears to me the Reverend Winslow has more on his mind than religion," countered Johnny, glad for the change of subject, willing the change to continue. "And I've never seen a man of God as handy with a gun as he seems to be. I saw him taking a potshot at a crow today. Knocked the poor creature clear out of the sky whilst flying. Then he just left it lying on the ground. I can't see any reason for killing God's creatures without a purpose."

"Must've justified it to his Maker as target practice," muttered Sam, squirming a little uncomfortably on his grain bag.

Maggie noticed. "Getting too tight in here for you, Sam?"

"No. Weren't that a'tall. Was just thinkin' on somethin' peculiar, somethin' the general direction of the conversation led me to remember. Wonderin' whether it be worth it to bring it up or not."

"Out with it, Thayer," urged Irish. "It's among friends you are."

"Just don't want to seem precipitate, is all." But now they were all staring at him and he was forced to continue. He cleared his throat. "Well, then . . . for all the recent rains, the ground's been a mess of mush constantly. Can't tell one impression from another—"

He had their attention.

" 'Cept under the overhang of my wagon, where it's parked of a night." He looked up. "It's sorta private territory, you know? Ought to have but my own footprints there, comin' in and goin' out."

"And?" nudged Johnny.

"Last few mornings, was another set of prints there as well. Male. Boots. Give me the impression someone's been spyin' on me."

"In your sleep?" Maggie was incredulous. "Couldn't it have been a neighbor seeking aid, then thinking better of it?"

"Two mornings in a row? Same set of prints?"

"Just thank the Lord they weren't moccasin prints!" Irish laughed nervously.

"My brother's right! It's the Indians we have to consider." Gwen was plainly worried.

"Nay, I'm bein' foolish. Must come of livin' alone too long. Just put it out of your minds. By and by, it'll be the train itself we have to worry about."

Sam had managed to gain their full attention. He'd spoken but few words all evening before his comments on the footprints, content just to warm himself and listen. Now his brow was furrowed with the unusual effort of expressing himself in company.

"I grew up in a village in Indiana. Learned my trade there from my daddy. Never been much for words. Maybe it was that the bellows and hammers always made too much noise for words. Did a lot of watchin' and learnin', though, about all kinds of critters—animal and human both." He stopped, perhaps perplexed by his verbosity.

"Yes, Sam?" prodded Maggie gently.

"For a community to work, has to have everybody pitchin' in, seems like."

"We all signed that westering constitution outside of Independence, Sam," threw in Irish.

"True. Swore on what we'd do, come catastrophe. To help each other. But with these rains, morale is fallin' apart already, and us hardly started. Just think of me and my silly fancies." He smiled to himself self-consciously, causing the ends of his huge mustache to turn up before putting his mind back to his thoughts.

"And we only done about five miles today. Got to be a lot more neighborly, like supper tonight, or things just gonna start to splinter. Everybody'll want to go his own way, fight over the little bit of kindling available, or look for a better trail, a faster cutoff." He pulled at his mustache.

"What we're doin' ain't so new. Santa Fe traders been haulin' wagons out for years without trouble. They're organized. Everybody got his own job, knows how to do it. Mountain men the same. Wouldn't be caught with the colds and dysentery already croppin' up, like us. We got to team up, or we'll be all wore out afore we get to Fort Laramie."

Maggie spoke first into the silence following Sam's speech. "Thank you for getting us out of the hole today, Sam."

Sam looked embarrassed, but Irish more so for having driven his teams past the Stuarts without offer of help.

There was a delicate pause before Sam filled it again. "Been sittin' here thinkin' on a proposition." He looked at Maggie. "Be mostly your decision, Maggie, since you'll bear the brunt of it if you accept." He looked at her wistfully, finally plunging ahead.

"I can handle my wagon and teams just fine, but the cookin' is a fair chore at day's end. And it gets lonesome-like, too, over a single campfire. Let me sup with you and I'll throw in more than my share of provisions, and see to your wagons and teams when they're needin' the help. I've a touch for the fixin' of things."

Maggie caught Johnny's eye. It was his decision, too. He'd be sharing his family's small period of privacy with a relative stranger. Both of them relished that brief time before turning in. On the other hand, God Himself knew that Johnny might be a man of dreams and words, a man of endless spirit, but pinch come to shove, he could barely keep the wagon wheels greased. Luckily, they hadn't needed much greasing yet. Then again, he'd learn how to do it if he had to. Think how he'd fixed up that water-logged press when he'd wanted to. . . . But on a trip like this, sometimes there wasn't the time for learning.

Sam saw the brief indecision and threw in his clincher. "Also I got some dry wood aboard. Might be enough to keep the stove goin' nights through another week of rain."

Maggie smiled. That offer was almost impossible to refuse. She glanced at Johnny again, searching for the assent she found in his eyes.

"What's one more mouth to feed?"

Irish assayed the new situation quickly. His most winning grin was presented. "Would the promise of a cabinful of crockery, your choice of glaze—delivered upon completion of my kiln in the Territory—buy Gwen and me a piece of this deal?"

Maggie caught Sam studying Gwen at this turn of affairs. Could there possibly be some interest there?

"Don't forget our provisions, Irish," added Gwen. "I'll even wash Charlotte's nappies, and sew up a new suit of clothes for each and every one of you come journey's end. You too, Sam."

Sam raised his thick eyebrows beneath his shaggy brown hair, and he cut a grin of his own, revealing strong white teeth. "Never had a personal seam-stress afore. Think you can fit these shoulders?" He stretched his bearlike body.

" 'And the muscles of his brawny arms are strong as iron bands,' " Maggie quoted.

They all laughed, and the pact was made. It left only Maggie to wonder how her "family" had so quickly expanded from four to seven.

five

At the next day's nooning, Johnny managed to pull their wagons over near a small outcrop of rock. Maggie eyed the boulders with interest. There was just enough ledge there to get a small fire going, out of the rains.

She called for Jamie, who was delighted to remove himself from another morning's confinement with the baby. "Hunt around underneath the rocks, son. See if you can find something dry for the fire. But be careful of snakes. Please?"

He was already off, with a whoop of pleasure.

Maggie entered the cabin where Charlotte was waiting, eager to be changed and fed. Maggie had dried some of the baby's linens on ropes strung around the cabin the night before, after the new covenant had been made. She pulled them down now, and launched into her next chore, cleaning and drying the grateful little one, taking the time to nuzzle her soft belly, to tweak her toes until the baby giggled with pleasure.

Charlotte was nursing when Jamie stormed into the cabin, his shirt oddly bulging. "Ma, Ma! I only saw one snake, a little black one, and got some dry brush for Pa. He's startin' up the fire and needs the coffeepot. Wait'll you see what else I found, though!"

Maggie rearranged the baby and got up. "What is it, Jamie?"

His shirt was opened for her inspection, presenting a very bedraggled ball of fur. It opened its eyes and whined heartrendingly.

As the wail increased in intensity, Johnny stuck his head through the door. "What about that coffeepot?" His eyes stopped on the damp bundle and he pulled himself in. "What have you found, son? Let me see."

Jamie passed over the ball. Small paws covered with fawn-colored fur scrabbled feebly at Johnny. Sharp little teeth went for his wrist.

"Ouch! Fierce little critter, and hungry, too. I do believe you've found yourself a coyote pup!" He frowned at the eager boy. "What about its mama? Don't you think she might miss him?"

"Nothing else in the den, Pa. It was cold and wet. And he was crying pitifullike."

Johnny carefully settled the creature atop a rag on the floor. "Show me where you found him, Jamie. And grab that coffeepot while you're at it. We've got to get some dinner going before the little bit of kindling we've got is burnt up."

Maggie finished feeding the baby, all the time listening to the pathetic cries from the new creature. Unable to stand its discomfort any longer, she settled Charlotte into her hammock and hauled out a slab of bacon, carefully cutting off a few tiny pieces. She presented these to the pup, who wolfed them down in short order. His immense eyes returned to hers, waiting for more.

"More? You want more? And it's bacon you crave, too. You've rich tastes, little one."

But she cut more for him, waited while it was consumed, then carefully toweled down the wet fur. When she left the wagon with bacon in a pan for her own family, the brazen creature was snuggled in a comfortable ball on the floor, fast asleep.

Her men returned with arms full of brush as the bacon was beginning to sizzle. She looked up at Johnny questioningly.

He shrugged his shoulders. "The den's been deserted. I found two other pups, farther back, both dead. Something must have happened to their mama."

Jamie was jiggling from one muddy foot to the other in great impatience. "May we keep him, Ma? Please? Pa said it was up to you, but I was to be completely responsible. And I will, too. It'll give me something to do while I'm sitting with Charley. I'll feed him. I can get some milk from the Krellers! And he can sleep with me, and—"

"I'm not sure we can afford him, Jamie. He's already taken a powerful interest in our bacon supply. We must think about feeding ourselves first."

"We'll be in buffalo country soon, Ma. I heard the men say so. There'll be enough meat for everyone then. Please, Ma!"

Jamie watched his mother weakening before his eyes. He waited no further for her answer, but raced into the cabin. In a few moments, though, he was out again, shamefaced, his hands behind his back.

"What is it, Jamie?"

Jamie held up a hunk of bacon. Fine little teethmarks had gnawed a considerable dent in one corner of the meat.

Maggie glanced at her husband, who was fighting off a huge grin. "Go ahead, Johnny. Say it."

"It seems like you've found yourself yet another orphan. Go keep Bacon out of further trouble, Jamie."

The rain had slowed to a soft drizzle, and Johnny had taken children and pup out for some air. Maggie was shoving Sam's firewood into the stove when Gwen knocked and walked in.

"I brought the onions you showed me how to pick for our supper, Maggie, and a pot of strawberry preserves. I wasn't sure what to do about flour and such—" She glanced around the crowded cabin evocatively.

"Space being what it is, we'd better work through our stock first, then borrow on yours. I was planning on more soup. And now that we've got the preserves, we can spread it on pancakes for a sweet."

"You certainly do know how to plan a meal!"

Maggie thought Gwen was teasing, then glanced at her face. No irony was involved. Her compliment had been offered in dead earnest.

"I seem to have trouble making decisions on things like meals, Maggie. I always have. I suppose I was never cut out to be a homemaker."

"Is that why you've never married?"

Gwen evaded the outright question. "Oh, it's not as if I've never run a household. I've raised Irish since he was eight. Our parents were taken off by the cholera, so there was little choice. I guess, it's the daily tediousness. . . . Back home, I finally worked out a pattern—baked beans on Monday, fowl on Tuesday, fowl pie on Wednesday, mutton on Thursday, fish on Friday. . . . You can't get any of that on the trail, regular-like, as you could in Boston—" She stopped at Maggie's barely hidden smile.

"May I give you some assistance?"

Maggie handed her a bowl. "Whip together a little pancake batter while I get the soup going." She watched as Gwen carefully placed the bowl on the tiny table and stared at it.

"About three cups of flour, Gwen, and a pinch of salt, a sprinkling of sugar, a pinch of salteratus for the rising, and water to mix. I'd use milk and eggs if we had them, but we don't."

"Oh."

Amusement and awe covered Maggie's face as Gwen began bumbling through the procedure. A woman who couldn't cook! Cooking had always come naturally to Maggie, growing up watching her mother as she had. She resisted the urge to shoo Gwen out and do it herself. It might be faster, but if the woman was to be any help at all, she'd just have to learn.

Maggie stirred her soup pot. "It's the food, then, that scared you off men?"

"No. . . ," Gwen hesitated. "It's the men. I'm used to Irish, and he's family, so he doesn't count. But other men. . . . They used to come calling, even proposing. Not so much now any more. At twenty-eight, I guess I'm past the marriageable age. It ought to be a relief, but sometimes I wonder."

She'd finally gotten the flour into the bowl and was hovering over it with a salt cake in her hand. "They just did not appeal to me, Maggie! So rough and forward they seemed. Is that so hard to understand? I got to thinking about living with them, day after day."

"The closeness frightens you?"

"Yes," Gwen finally admitted. She reached for the sugar bag. "Is there something wrong with me, Maggie?"

Maggie carefully cut around the slab of bacon, where the pup had chewed at it, throwing a clean piece into her warming water.

"More likely you were courted by the wrong men. I haven't that much experience myself. I've never been courted by anyone but Johnny. Never wanted anyone but Johnny. But Johnny I wanted. From the first." She smiled in remembrance of Johnny's wagon coming round the bend when she was ten, of Johnny himself, laughing and mischievous, asking if he could water his horse. Of Johnny unlatching the rear door of this very wagon to haul out his ancient and inebriated father. The soup pot began to bubble before her eyes, pulling her memories into its whirlpool.

"When the right kind of man comes along, you'll find it a pleasure to be near him, Gwen. Love opens a woman up like a flower, it does." She stopped and sighed, spoon in hand, still thinking about Johnny.

Gwen watched her expression wistfully. "It can still happen? Even at twenty-eight?"

"I do believe it can happen at any age, Gwen."

"I'd surely love to look on someone the way you

look on your Johnny. And have him return the same look."

"It will happen. A woman who has the appearance you do oughtn't to be wasted. I hear there're all sorts of men in the Territory just crying out for good wives." She laughed. "But they'll want someone who can cook, Gwen. You'd better throw a little more flour into that batter. You've about drowned it out with water."

Gwen colored, but did as she was instructed.

They were all stuffed into the cabin again, finishing their soup. Maggie squeezed past the men and reached for the platter of pancakes. She'd spread preserves on them, and carefully rolled them up with a sprinkling of sugar on top. She'd known a Frenchwoman in Chicago who served them like that, calling them some kind of a foreign name. She couldn't remember the name, but it still came down to pancakes, and they did look prettier that way.

Maggie presented the sweet with a flourish. "Gwen made the dessert."

Sam's eyes took on a glint of interest, and he reached for two. Maggie and Gwen both waited, Gwen with an anxious frown, as he bit into the first and began to chew solemnly. The surprise in the center startled him, and he let out a slow smile. "Good," he pronounced, and reached for another.

Gwen blushed.

Jamie poked his head down from the upper bunk. "How about me, Ma? They look past delicious!"

"Did you finish your soup, Jamie?"

"Sure. That is, all but a very tiny bit, and Bacon's doing that in right now."

Heads rose to watch Bacon almost lost in Jamie's soup bowl, his tail wagging with enthusiasm. Feeding him was to be no problem. He'd eat anything available. Maggie laughed with the rest, and passed around the remainder of the dessert.

Johnny put his empty bowl down first. "How's the footprint situation today, Sam?"

It was Sam's turn to blush. "Must've been a figment, like I said. Things was clean as a whistle this mornin'."

"What footprints?" demanded Jamie.

"This is grown-up talk, son. Did I hear anyone invite you to partake of it?"

"No, sir." Chagrined, the boy turned his attention back to the pup.

Johnny was taking no chances with little pitchers and their big ears, however. All Jamie had to do was report a few words of the conversation to his friends, and those words would spread like wildfire, creating rumors of sneaking Indians or Mormons or both. Time to change the subject.

"I was talking to Max Kreller before supper tonight, showing off the pup to his brood. He spotted a small herd of deer this evening, just before we stopped. There might be some good meat nearby for the hunting."

The other men looked up in interest. You could almost see venison steaks floating before their eyes.

"How do we get 'em?" asked Sam practically.

"Exactly. We need a plan."

six

The Kansas River had to be crossed. It was eighty-seven miles out of Independence. As first emigrants of the season, the Chandler Party's early arrival had given the swollen river little time to calm itself.

When they came to the Pappan Ferry at midmorning, Captain Chandler ordered the wagons to line themselves up. Johnny unyoked and tethered the Stuarts' oxen, and the whole family walked to the river's edge to watch with the rest of the emigrants as the process began.

Maggie peered over the edge of the bank first. "Johnny! It looks dangerous!" she gasped, and automatically reached to feel for Charlotte on her back and firmly grasp Jamie's hand.

Johnny's reaction to the sight was quite different. "The Kansas must be two hundred yards wide! And the currents are running mean! Something real is happening at last." A grin of anticipation spread across his face. "Watch! They're testing the waters with Chandler's wagon."

The captain's white-top was being lowered down the steep bank by means of a rope, one end winched around a stout tree. It was slow work. Waiting below was a very curious concoction of a boat.

"What kind of a raft is that, Johnny? I never saw one like it on the Ohio."

"It looks like two pirogues—canoes—bridged with poles, Meg. I think they mean to float the

71

wagon in the middle."

Maggie shivered in the early spring warmth. Johnny noticed and gave her hand a firm squeeze. "Not to worry, love. The owners of the ferry—those two Indian-looking gentlemen directing the proceedings down there—they've been doing this since '44. The Pappan brothers. Their father was a French mountain man, their mother a squaw. They're in the guidebooks, and Chandler seems comfortable with them."

Maggie studied the sweep of water, surging powerfully against its banks. "Where's Jamie?" She spun around wildly. He'd slipped out of her grasp unnoticed. In her mind's eye, the boy had already fallen into the waters and was even now being swallowed irrevocably by the merciless currents.

"Rest easy, Meg. He's wandered over there, with the Kreller girls." Johnny pointed.

Maggie ignored the creaks and groans of the Chandler wagon being lowered against its will. "I'm off to get him into my sights."

Johnny smiled. "This should be an easy crossing, Meg. We've a ferry to help us. A thousand miles beyond here is when you can begin to worry."

"I still mean to keep that boy firmly in view. The way he hops around, he could be vaulting himself into the river any moment. He's overly impressed with himself and his exploits these days, I'm thinking. And if he fell in, even his strong swimming couldn't save him from those currents!"

Johnny shrugged. "Maybe you're right. I guess I forget the boy's only seven." And Johnny himself stepped nearer to the brink.

Maggie caught up with Jamie in the center of a crowd of youngsters. He was busily scratching something on a bare patch of earth with a stone.

Finished, he stood up importantly to show off his work. "There, Matty. This is how I see it. That big old rope is acting like a pulley, levering the wagon's weight slowly down—" He sensed something and looked up. " 'Lo, Ma, Charley. Just explaining to the girls how the ferrying business works. Wish I knew the depth of the river so I could judge how those Injuns figure to pole the wagons across."

Maggie let out her pent-up breath. Maybe he had more sense than she gave him credit for.

"You must be Jamie's mother. Good boy you've got there."

Maggie collected herself to stare up into the calm eyes of a finc-looking, chestnut-haired man.

He smiled at her, clamped his teeth down on his meerschaum pipe, and held out a hand. "I'm Max Kreller, Matty's father. And Hilda's, and Irene's, too. She's the baby."

Maggie smiled back. "I've heard nothing but 'Matty this and Matty that' since the trip began. The children do seem to have taken to each other."

He nodded his head in agreement. "Matilda don't take to many, so it's a pleasure to see them get on like that. Always wanted to be a boy, she has."

"She'll grow out of it when the time is ripe. A pleasure to meet you, Mr. Kreller."

"Max."

"Maggie Stuart, Max."

A slight woman bustled up, a baby near Charlotte's age draped over one shoulder, busily pulling fistfuls of dark black hair out of her mother's bun. "You Jamie's mother?"

She didn't wait for Maggie's nod of agreement. "I've been wanting awful bad to meet up with you. I'm Hazel, Max's wife, and mother to his daughters." She went on, nonstop. "I do admire the way you've dealt with your baby, slung on your back like that. Ain't never seen nothing like that back in Pennsylvania where we come from. Looks a mite easier'n how I handle mine, and leaves your hands freed up for the work, too."

"I learned it from my Indian friends in Independence." Maggie watched Hazel's eyes widen in surprise. "If you've got a length of extra canvas and a few sticks, I could fix you up the same."

"Would you? I'd be much obliged, and that's the truth!"

"Sure you don't mind a little learning from the 'heathen'?" teased Maggie gently.

Hazel grunted. "Sounds like you've met up with that parson Winslow. Beats me how a slew of Christians can send someone so full of himself out to the missions. Plenty of decent ministers back home don't look down their noses at every blessed soul. And the way he's been going on about Mormons to any that'll listen! He'd have my eyes turned 'round clear to my back if I hadn't already decided to swallow less than half of what he says."

Maggie laughed. "I think we're going to be friends, Hazel."

"Don't see why not. We seem to be close to the same age and all. We got youngsters the same, and husbands with wanderlust the same. There's a lot we could share. I just did for the cows, so why don't I get you a nice cup of milk?"

When the Kreller family took their turn at the ferry, baby Irene was trussed up on her mother's back like Charlotte. Maggie stood watching, heart in throat, as her new friends helped to ease their wagon onto the frail-looking raft and climbed aboard. Hazel shaded her eyes to wave at Maggie. "See you 'tother side. Come 'round for some more milk after you've made land!"

Maggie waved harder. It would be their turn soon. She looked around for Johnny. He'd finally wearied of watching the proceedings and was comfortably ensconced under a nearby tree, reading a book as if nothing were happening.

Jamie raced up and screeched to a halt. "May I have a book, too, Ma? The girls are gone across. The Richmans and Jube—they've gone, too. There's no one to play with."

Maggie motioned toward a group of wan children, scrabbling in the muddy wagon ruts nearby. "What about them?"

Jamie gave a deprecating shake of his head. "They're Winslows. You know their pa don't 'low them to mix."

Maggie sighed. "You're way behind on your lessons anyway."

"It's not lessons I'm after, Ma. I've memorized

enough poems through this past rainy spell to last me forever. Pa says we're on *sab-bat-i-cal*, after all. I'm looking for some adventure!"

"Poems are fun. You can't ever memorize enough of them. You'll not be avoiding your serious lessons for the whole trip, my boy. Take those multiplication tables, for instance—"

"I'd rather leave 'em, Ma."

Maggie's tone brooked no nonsense. "Ja-mie! Three times nine is. . . ?"

"Umm." He stood twitching his fingers, obviously counting up on them. "Twenty-six?"

"My point in a nutshell." Maggie shook her head. "I'll have to talk to your father about this. And as for that adventure business, it seems to me there could be few things more adventurous than what you've been watching here all day."

"It palls after a while, it does. A person like me needs excitement every minute!"

"Young man, I was never entertained every moment of my childhood. In fact, I can't remember *ever* being entertained."

"It couldn't have been *that* bad on the farm, Ma."

Maggie had to laugh in spite of herself. "I guess it wasn't, at that." Her eyes went from Jamie right over to the far side of the Kansas River without seeing it. The farm hadn't been bad at all. Not after Johnny started coming each year to their cabin with his father and their books. She thought again of her parents left behind on their parcel of land near the banks of the Ohio River. Her mild-mannered, sweet mother; her stern, red-headed father whose only

peace was found in constant work and regular read-
ings of the Scripture; her sister and three brothers. It
seemed too long since she'd laid eyes on them.

"Is it all right, Ma?" Jamie's question brought her
back to the present.

"What?"

"To get a book!"

Exasperated, Maggie gave up the struggle. "Certainly, Jamie."

She eased herself down near her husband to feed
the baby. It would have been better if they'd been
right up in front of the line like the Chandlers.
There'd have been no waiting and worry all the day.
What would her own mother think if she could see
Maggie now, ready to endanger everything she held
dear in this world, all for the fording of a river in
flood? Her mother had never been farther than thirty
miles from the farm, to camp meeting every autumn.
She'd never understand, not even with the letters
Maggie had been sending from Independence.

The sounds of the rope winching down another
groaning wagon broke into Maggie's thoughts. The
Krellers had made it across, all right. So had everyone else. The two half-breed brothers seemed to
know their business. They'd certainly had enough
practice. She ought to just relax—

"It's swamped! Ma! Pa! They've lost a wagon!"

Jamie's book landed in the dust, and Charlotte
clung to Maggie with an alarmed expression as
Maggie and Johnny raced for the bank. Once there,
Maggie's eyes traveled unerringly to the spot where
the white-top was turned on its side, rushing down-

stream with the currents.

Slowly, too slowly, hands reached out from within to grasp at the canvas. One by one children, wife and husband were clinging to the top of the wagon, still tearing downstream.

"Who are they?"

"The Butlers," whispered Jamie. "Ain't had much to do with them so far. Guess I won't, either."

"Haven't," corrected Johnny. His excitement over the flooding river was gone. He reached one arm around Maggie, the other around Jamie. "There's nothing easy in this life, son. Remember. Pray for them. When we're across, we'll track them down and see what aid we can offer."

Too soon, the ferrymen were back in business as if nothing had happened. Then it was the Stuarts' turn.

Johnny helped his family down the slope and slowly counted out four one-dollar coins into the nearest Pappan's hand. When he was finished, the hand was still outstretched. Johnny looked up.

"It be another twenty-five cents each animal, and ten cents each man. Throw in the papoose, no charge."

Johnny counted out more coins.

"Do we get our money back if we swamp like the Butlers?" Jamie asked, giving the ferrymen a shrewd look.

The taller of the two men, stripped to the waist, coal-black hair wet and slicked back, stared at the boy and finally broke into a brown-stained smile. "For you, maybe we give half back. T'other family ain't had the sense to ask beforetimes. Told 'em they was top-heavy."

"We ain't—aren't—top-heavy, are we Pa?" Jamie frowned at Johnny.

Johnny turned to one of the brothers questioningly.

The half-breed spat out a stream of tobacco juice. "Iffen you had problems, I'd a said so. You be holdin' up the line."

Johnny straightened his shoulders. "Go ahead with the children, Meg. I'll come across with the books." He gave them each a hug as he planted them firmly inside the canvas top. "See you before you know it."

Maggie sat on an edge of the dismantled Ramage printing press, grasping the little brass finial of its top piece like a talisman. It had been beneath the waters of a great river once before. Surely once was more than enough.

Charlotte, firmly strapped to her back, was blessedly napping. Jamie was sharing his mother's perch, clinging to her free hand tightly. His face magnified her own fear. True adventure was better in books. She was afraid to look forward, afraid to look back. But she'd have to do something for the boy.

"Can you unbutton that side flap, Jamie? Let in some river breeze. We can watch the Pappans pole us across. You wondered how they did it, after all. We might even pick up a few pointers for future crossings."

Jamie loosed his death grip and did as bidden. Then he was back, holding her less tightly. "We've shoved off, Ma! We're floating now! Can you feel it?"

"Yes." Maggie tried to control the quaver in her voice. "Yes, I certainly do feel it." It was a strange sort of a floating sensation, the wagon swaying and complaining in ways it was unused to. It made her feel completely out of control. The trail might be hard, but at least it kept her feet firmly on the solid earth.

"Long time since we've been on the water, Ma. Remember when we crossed the Mississippi after Nauvoo? Just after Charley was born, that was, and Pa expecting a posse from Carthage on our backs the whole time 'cause we'd consorted with the Mormon doctor, or maybe even a posse of Mormons on account of the press." His forehead wrinkled a moment at the thought of two posses potentially after them before he leaped ahead. " 'Course, the ferry was considerably bigger there, almost like a real boat. Then there was the one on the Missouri, before we got to wintering in Independence—"

"You remember all that, Jamie?"

He was insulted. "It was only last year, Ma!"

Maggie smiled. "You're so right. I forget what a young man you're becoming. Especially since your last birthday."

She forced herself to peek through the arched canvas opening ahead of them. They were approaching the shore at an angle. It must be the currents. But the far bank did seem to be coming closer. They might even be halfway across. "There will be many more rivers to ford on this trip, Jamie, but I doubt any of them will be as deep as this."

"I know, and they've got nice names, too. *Platte.*

Snake. Imagine naming a river *snake*." He chuckled, and ventured another look through the side flap. "Ma! I can see Dickens and Miss Sally! They're swimming for all they're worth, and don't look too happy. And there's Brandy and Duke coming up. Buster is way over to the side. Looks like he might land a fair piece downstream. Can't see Checkers or the rest, though. Boy, oh, boy, but aren't we going to have a time rounding them all up when Pa follows us!"

Maggie gave her son a hug. He was getting her across, not the other way around. She stared through the side opening with him. She could see the to-bacco-chewing Pappan leaning into his pole from his perch in the canoe. His hairless chest was glossy with sweat and spray, and glistened a fine bronze in the sun. He was worth the six dollars and change.

Almost before she realized it, they were bumping softly into the far bank. The ferrymen were hooking them to teams of oxen to pull them up the slope, through the quarter mile of sandy flats to solid land and the waiting wagons of the train beyond. Maggie sent a heartfelt "Thank You" to the heavens until she could more properly express her gratitude at evening devotions.

By the time their wagon was settled with the others, Johnny would be almost across with the caravan. She wouldn't even think about his following the Butlers downstream.

Everyone still fording the river made it. Then there was the stock to catch. Johnny took off with the other men after their animals. The women used the time and the river to catch up on their washing. By dark, each white-top was covered with freshly laundered clothing and linens, spread out to catch the breezes.

Maggie had the children asleep when Johnny finally returned with the last of the oxen. He tethered them to graze and wearily stopped at his own hearth, accepting the coffee and food she'd kept warming for him.

"It's rice for a change. I thought you might like it. I fried it with wild onions and a little bacon. Has it gotten too dry?"

He offered a smile through his full mouth and swallowed. "Ambrosial."

"Johnny, your father always used to say that." Maggie felt tears welling up at the sudden memory of the old man. The day had been too long. She brushed at her eyes. The obvious could no longer be ignored. "What happened to the Butlers, Johnny?"

He reached for his cup and tasted the coffee.

"Tell me, Johnny. I'm twenty. A grown woman. I can take it."

"I never promised the trip would be easy, Meg. Thank the Lord, the Butler family was all spared. Cold and wet, but spared. Their wagon and all their belongings were finished, though. The heavy stuff just sank to the bottom of the river. The rest floated off, the wagon splintered in pieces. When we found them, they were on the other side of the river, their animals to this side. We had to drive the beasts back again when the Butlers refused another crossing.

Two of the oxen didn't make it."

He paused, remembering. "Seems one of the beasts was a particular pet of the children. It was the final straw. The whole lot of youngsters just broke down in tears, and their mother, too." Johnny made an effort to finish the story with as little emotion as possible.

Maggie knew it was not from a lack of feeling, just his way of trying to deal with it.

"The men took up a collection. We got enough to get them back to Independence and maybe a little beyond. They should make it fast, unfettered by the wagon. Last I saw, they were walking toward the east, mighty chastened." He picked up his spoon again.

Maggie watched him eat with studied concentration. It could have been her family. Or the Hardistys or the Krellers. There would be no singing in the camp tonight.

seven

Maggie saw her first wild Indians three mornings later. There were two of them, lounging on their ponies on a small rise overlooking the camp.

She froze.

Tame Indians in Independence were one thing. Half-breeds, like the Pappas brothers at the Kansas River crossing, were another. But real, *wild* Indians! Beyond the territorial United States, in the middle of nowhere, her calmness evaporated. She turned tail and rushed back into the wagon.

"Johnny!"

Her husband was blearily pulling braces over his shoulders, trying to dress without waking the children.

Maggie lowered her voice. "Johnny!" She pointed outdoors.

He caught the expression on her face, picked up his boots, and followed.

"On the rise, through the mist. Look."

He looked. The Indians were carrying muskets, and their bearing was insolent as they watched the camp come alive before them.

Johnny pulled on his boots with more urgency than before. "I'm going after Chandler. You might as well get on with the breakfast. There are only two of them, so they can't mean us harm."

Maggie started in on her chores, but felt a constant prickle rising and descending through her spine. She suddenly understood how Sam had felt about his unexplained footprints, footprints that had turned up a third time. To be spied on secretly must be even worse. Far worse. At least, these Indians would present their demands openly when they were good and ready.

She turned around with feigned nonchalance to give the two men another glance. They were carrying their firearms in a peculiar, cautionary way, the breech held in the right hand and the barrel resting on the left, as if at any moment they would be raised and fired. The thought did not ease her. Neither did their headdress. The men were shaven almost bald, with stiff tufts of hair rising from the nape of the neck to the forehead like cock's combs.

Something came back to Maggie. Her friend Flower Blossom, back in Independence, had been a Kansas Indian, and Flower Blossom's husband Black Raven had worn a headdress like this the one time they'd met. These men must be Kansas, or *Caw*. And everyone knew that was a friendly tribe, practically civilized. She ventured another peek at the two. At the moment they didn't *look* civilized.

Maggie got the fire going. Smoke drifting past her face, she stood and watched as a small delegation approached the braves—Captain Chandler and Johnny, Max Kreller and Sam, along with several other men. She held her breath while both Indians raised their right arms to the approaching men.

Charlotte chose that moment to let out a roar of hunger. Maggie remained transfixed, trying to follow the unfolding scene until Jamie climbed out of the wagon, rubbing his eyes.

"Charley's awful hungry, Ma. She woke me up."
Then he saw what she was watching. "Injuns! Real
ones! Whooee!"

Before she could grab him by his shirttails, Jamie
was gone, racing barefoot through the camp. At
least he had the sense to stop at the edge and wait
with the growing crowd of spectators. Maggie went
after her squalling baby.

The morning's start was delayed by the Indian
visit.

Johnny had finally returned to his own campfire
and was downing his breakfast with excitement.
"We got to see some natural Indians, at last! It
means we're coming into interesting territory. Can't
wait till we get beyond the Caws' lands, though!"

Maggie could wait, with pleasure, but wasn't
about to drench Johnny's enthusiasm. He'd been
talking Indians to her since he'd been old enough to
understand Rousseau's essays on the "truly natural
man." Not that Rousseau had ever set foot out of
Europe to see one of his specimens.

"What did they come for, Johnny?"

"One of them had no flint for his gun. He wanted
one. Chandler says they probably slipped it out on
purpose, to get another, but we scrounged up a flint
nonetheless."

Jamie, crouched next to Johnny and his mother,
was listening to the story avidly.

"Then they signified that they wanted something
to put in their cook pans. So we bribed 'em with a

chunk of bacon and a little flour for their leathern bags, and they left."

"Was that all?"

"Everything. Except for the initial 'How, How.' " He gulped down another bite of his pan-fried bread. "Chandler figures they're just checking us out. He says we ought to start camping in a circle of wagons from here out. And post lookouts, too. We'll have to get up some volunteers. Stock starts disappearing oppressingly often from this point on."

"From this point . . . until when, Johnny?"

Johnny smiled at Maggie's wail. " 'Til about the end of the line."

"Oh, Johnny, haven't you seen enough of the elephant yet?"

"*What* elephant?" Jamie wanted to know. "I thought elephants only grew in darkest Africa."

Johnny grinned. "It's a figure of speech, son. A way of talking about new, unseen wonders a person's got a hankering for."

"I'd sure be able to work up a hankering to see a real elephant, Pa."

"You're going to have to settle for real Indians and buffalo, Jamie." Johnny reached for his son's head and tousled it. "Although I did see a real elephant once."

"Really?"

"Yes. Not much older than you, I was. My pa took me to see it when we were wintering in New York one year. Paid a whole quarter to get me in for the sight. He called it a 'necessary educational expense.' It was quite an impressive creature, but I'll warrant it won't hold a candle to a herd of buffalo."

Jamie was a little miffed at having missed the elephant opportunity. "That remains to be seen, Pa."

Johnny got up. "What needs to be seen now is the stock. Grab a bridle and help me collect Dickens and Miss Sally. They're growing fat and lazy with all this good green grass. We'll have to take the time to give them a workout soon."

Maggie began cleaning up after the meal, Indians, elephants, and buffalo floating through her head. What an extraordinary world it was, after all.

eight

Johnny had a chance to exercise Dickens sooner than he anticipated. It was midafternoon when a cry rose from the head of the train and traveled quickly through its length.

"Elk! Elk!"

"Broiled steaks!"

"Ribs!"

"Fresh meat!"

Maggie raised her head and peered through the haze. There was a definite dark cloud, a moving one, off to the north of the train. Farther west was another dark area, more spread out, but stationary. She fervently prayed it was a copse of trees. Their need for firewood was acute. They hadn't yet come into buffalo country, the country that would give them the chips Johnny had mentioned as fuel for most of their journey. . . .

"Jamie!" Johnny was yelling for their son.

The boy bounded out of nowhere and went to relieve his father. In a moment, Johnny was trotting toward Maggie.

"Did you hear that, Meg? Did you see?"

She smiled at his excitement. "Elk meat would be welcome, Johnny."

He hardly stopped. "Got to get my gun. Got to talk to Chandler. Get a hunting party up. I'll be back."

Maggie doggedly kept the oxen advancing. It looked like the women and children were going to

89

have to keep the train going. She glanced behind her. Irish had handed his whip to Gwen and was feverishly trying to saddle and bridle a horse. The menfolk were reacting the same way all up and down the line, except for Sam. With no wife or child to relieve him, he continued to plod along as steadily as the women, untouched by the commotion.

Soon Johnny was galloping back, astride Dickens. "Make for that grove of trees up ahead, Meg. We're going to camp down early today for the hunt. Chandler says it's the Big Vermillion Creek, with the last stand of real hardwood we're likely to see in a while. You women will have to set up camp on this side. Get Jamie to collect as much wood as he can while I'm gone."

He paused only long enough to reach down and swing Maggie off her feet in a bone-crushing hug. Then he kissed her for luck, and was off, riding like one of the wild Indians of the plains, primed for the hunt.

The women of the train began to settle their wagons in a very tentative circle next to the trees and water of the Big Vermillion. It was easier said than done. The oxen, heedless of their heavy yokes and burdens, had already smelled the water and were lunging for it, eager to drink their fill.

"Brandy! Stop that! Duke!" Maggie wielded her whip in an effort to make the oxen turn. "Gee! Turn right, I say, not left! Gee!"

Behind her, Gwen was yelling "Haw." *Gees* and

Haws and thwacks resounded through the wagons until Hazel shouted from across the semicircle, "I give up!"

So did the other women. Whips were dropped and yokes "manhandled" by gasping females. Finally freed, the stock showed more enthusiasm than they had all day in their dash toward the creek bank.

Maggie flopped onto the grass, heaving. How easy to forget the usefulness of men with their natural strength. When her pulse rate almost slowed to normal, she finally raised her head into the brilliant sky. The sun was heading westward. It must be almost three. Its strong and welcome rays were already beginning to dry up the mud surrounding them.

Her other duties borne upon her by a yell from Charlotte, Maggie forced herself up to go after a ground sheet and the baby. The little one was ready for liberation, too.

"You ladies surely were a sight, Ma, sweating and thwacking like you were!"

Maggie wheeled around, baby in arms. "Jamie! I completely forgot you were dealing with your father's wagon. How did you get it so nicely curved in front of mine?"

Jamie grinned. "It was nothing, Ma."

"Don't you go exaggerating into fibs with me, young man. Remember what happened to George Washington when he was your age."

"Wasn't fibbing, Ma. It wasn't nothing a *man* couldn't do."

Maggie took in the thrust-out chest, the cocky

stance of the tow-headed boy. She bit back her own grin. "All right, then, young sir. Since those yokes are like feathers in your hands, you can help me build a corral out of them for your sister. So she can exercise, but not crawl off to get into mischief."

"Aw, Ma. I got man's work to do—"

He still wasn't too old to nab by the collar.

Jamie helped to build the tiny corral around the ground sheet. He forgot himself and his new importance long enough to tickle his sister's toes before his duties came back to him.

"Where's my special hatchet, Ma?"

"It should be with the tools in your father's wagon."

Jamie ran off, to return swinging the tool like a sword.

"For heaven's sake, watch how you handle that, son. Keep away from fingers."

"Yes, Ma."

"Your own and others!"

"Yes, Ma."

Maggie relented. "And don't forget George Washington. Watch out for cherry trees!"

"Aren't any cherry trees out here on the prairie, Ma—" He finally caught her joke and laughed. Charlotte giggled at his mirth, and he reached into her corral for one more tickle before racing off with his little hatchet into the trees, Bacon scampering after him.

Maggie sat with the baby for a few minutes, letting the warmth of the sun ease her tired muscles. The early stopping was a delight, but she knew she couldn't squander the gifts of fair weather and time. There were too many needs pressing upon her. Leaving Charlotte with a little soft, stuffed doll she'd made for her to teethe on, Maggie went into the book wagon to collect dirty linens. The creek was a ready-made laundry site, and she had washing galore crying out for the job.

Other women had already gathered by the side of the creek. Maggie nodded hello to Grandma Richman, and to the Reverend Winslow's wife—a pale, long-suffering looking woman—then threw down her parcel of soiled linens and her thick brown soap next to Hazel Kreller.

Hazel grinned hello. "Your man gone off half crazy like my Max?"

Maggie laughed. "I surely hope they shoot something. Just one elk would make a nice meal for the camp tonight. But I'm not counting my chickens. Even though he's practiced at targets, and actually bagged some small game back in Independence, Johnny's never aimed a gun at anything as impressive as an elk in his life. It would be a miracle if he actually hit something."

Hazel nodded knowingly. "Hopefully not each other, either." She moved to offer Maggie a spot on the broad, flat boulder she was using as a washboard to pound her clothes, then spun her head around as only a mother can do when attuned to her small children. "Hilda! Now I told you to look after baby Irene. Carry her away from that slope!"

Maggie glanced back. "Want to put Irene in Charlotte's corral? Then Hilda could go off with the rest of the children after firewood. That's where she probably wants to be anyhow."

"Hilda's but four and a half, Maggie."

"She shouldn't get into too much mischief with the others to look after her."

Hazel wiped her soapy forearms on her skirts. "You're probably right at that. She'll find more mischief here ignoring the baby. I'd best go get her settled."

In Hazel's absence, Maggie took a pile of scrubbed linens down to deeper water to be rinsed. Mrs. Winslow was there already, and started at Maggie's approach.

"Not to worry. I surely won't bite. I'm Maggie Stuart, and I've been meaning to be a little more neighborly." She thrust out a wet, soapy hand.

The preacher's wife hesitated for several heartbeats before taking Maggie's fingers in her own. "Ruth Winslow."

" 'Whither thou goest, I will go; and where thou lodgest, I will lodge: thy people shall be my people, and thy God my God,' " Maggie quoted. "You've a fitting name for a missionary's wife."

"Would that I could bear up as well as my namesake!"

Maggie was taken by the catch in the woman's voice. She studied more closely the faded blond hair, the washed-out blue eyes that surely had held a sparkle in the past. Ruth Winslow, perhaps thirty-five, seeming more like fifty, had once been an attractive woman.

Maggie spoke more gently. "Surely with a

preacher husband, you're used to the road. It can't be all that different from being married to a peddler, as I am."

"We weren't always on the road. And my husband wasn't always as he appears now. Once we had a lovely church, a joyous congregation. . . . It was such a pleasant, bounteous town for the boys to grow in, before the troubles. Illinois—" She stopped suddenly, as if realizing that she'd revealed far too much.

Maggie tried to gloss over her remarks, to make the woman more comfortable. "The Oregon country is said to be lovely, too. You'll have a church again, and a congregation."

"Of Indians! I fear them more than the Mor—" She stopped again. Stopped cold and picked up her washing. White-faced, she gave Maggie a curt nod and disappeared up the slope of the bank.

Maggie stared after Ruth Winslow in astonishment. What was that all about? And what had she almost spit out? Mor . . . Mormons? What had the Winslows to fear from the Mormons? And why?

Maggie mulled over the conversation as she finished her rinsing. When Hazel returned, Maggie put Ruth Winslow and her troubles out of her mind, as she had put the woman's husband and his peculiarities out of mind so often before. With Hazel, she spent a pleasant afternoon, gossiping while pounding and wringing the mud of travel from their wash.

At sunset the circle of wagons was draped in drying laundry. Big piles of gathered fuel were growing before each campsite when the sounds of hoofbeats were at last heard echoing over the plains.

Maggie looked up from the fire she was preparing. She figured she'd at least get the coffee going, but had been at a loss as to how to handle the meal itself. Was she to wait for promised meat? Would there be any?

She swooped Charlotte into her arms and trailed after the rest of the women and children to the far edge of camp, anxious to learn what had happened.

Irish galloped in first and swung off his saddle in a most dashing manner. He landed directly in front of Josh Chandler's daughter Susan, an attractive young lady of about sixteen. Susan gazed into his eyes with an expression bordering on idolatry. Maggie noted the possible ramifications with a small chuckle to herself before listening to what Irish was saying.

"We got three—a huge buck that must weigh fifteen hundred pounds, and two smaller females! Made up some pallets to drag 'em back. The men said to get the fires going. There'll be a celebration tonight, for sure!"

The women smiled, the children cheered, and Maggie returned to enlarge her fire. Next, with Jamie's help, she began to build a few drying racks with the branches the boy had collected. That much meat would spoil quickly if it wasn't preserved.

Hazel and Gwen wandered over to watch her at work. "What you fixing to do, Maggie?"

"The meat will probably be divided among families, so I'm going to smoke some jerky with our extras, Hazel. It'll be tough as leather, but it will keep. And it will taste good when we're hungry on the trail."

Ruth Winslow appeared on the edge of their group. She gave the other women a tentative, tired smile.

Maggie thought that maybe she was trying to apologize for her earlier behavior, so she made room for the missionary's wife around the circle. "I'm just giving a demonstration on how to dry meat like my Indian friends back in Independence taught me. Want to join the class?"

Ruth Winslow paled and almost sprang away. She had to be the most skittish creature Maggie had ever met. But she was also obviously trying hard to overcome some of her fears, now that her husband was not back yet to keep her under his stern gaze.

"I . . . I daren't. My husband would rather his family starve than eat what the *heathens* do."

Maggie looked up at her. "Which is worse—to die of starvation, or to learn how to survive from people who have mastered the art? We'd be foolish to ignore the wisdom of the Indians. Besides, it might help you to understand them better when you live among them."

"You may be right." Ruth glanced around quickly, as if to be sure she was not being overhead. "But the Reverend, my husband, says the Lord will provide. Oh, I wish—" Then she bolted for her own campsite like one of the animals the men had hunted.

Maggie caught the sudden flash of sympathy in Hazel's eyes and said, "The Lord helps those who help themselves, in more ways than one. I'm just grateful I'm not married to a man like that!"

Gwen nodded and rushed to change the subject. "I'd better get another fire going, Maggie, so I can smoke some, too. May I borrow a little wood?"

Maggie nodded yes to Gwen.

Hazel still lingered. "Only thing I'm dead set against is having my family starve," she said. "What would you judge to be the proper distance from the fire to smoke the meat?"

Laughing, Maggie showed her, adding, "It's a little early in the season yet, but if you should see any fresh berries along the way—strawberries, maybe—start collecting and drying them, Hazel. When you get enough, I'll teach you how to make pemmican out of the jerky, berries, and a little animal lard."

"I surely do appreciate your free-will advice, Maggie. I'll send Matty by with some more milk for you. Just don't let Jamie squander too much of it on that wild animal of his!"

The moon shone on their little party for the first time in days as they sat, replete with elk steaks. The Stuart family had received a liver, too, since one of their party had actually bagged an animal. Maggie had fried that up first, making sure that each of them ate a fair share of the healthful organ. Now the seven of them were spread around the fire, Johnny occasionally stirring himself to rotate the thin slivers of meat smoking above it.

Irish belched comfortably. "Chandler's called a

halt for tomorrow. A free day to rest up the stock, make repairs, and deal with the meat."

Maggie shifted the sleeping baby in her lap. "That sounds like pure heaven. Have we really been on the road for over two weeks?"

"Yup," from someone.

Jamie raised his nodding head. "Tell me again how you got the elk, Pa. Wisht I'd been along."

"In another few years, you'll be able to do just that, son."

"Always another few years. Why am I never the right age now?"

"It will come in the fullness of time." Johnny laughed. "But you know it wasn't me that shot the poor beast. Even after all the fine hunting plans we'd made, we were floundering around till Sam joined us late, after he docked his wagon." Johnny laid a hand on Sam's shoulder. "You took in the situation mighty fast, friend."

"What'd Sam do, Pa?"

"Just used his good sense, Jamie. Suggested we cut a buck out of the herd. Max joined the three of us and together we did just that. We tired him out and Sam made the kill. It was the Reverend Winslow himself who shot a second. The man's got eyes like a hawk. Sam's kill was tidier, but Winslow, he let off a shot from an impossible distance, and made it good." He leaned back against the wagon, relaxed and satiated. "We ought to start up a saga about all this, like Homer or the Vikings."

"Who be Homer?" Sam asked a little suspiciously.

"Just a poet who lived back in the times of the

ancient Greeks. He wrote up the history of their battles in verse. Interesting stuff. It reminds you that men don't change much over the years."

"I think I'd rather have a song, Pa," Jamie decided. "It would be nice under the stars."

Johnny smiled. "The Greeks used to sing their poems, too, Jamie. But to the music of a lyre, not a banjo. Still, the banjo is sort of appropriate for our story. What should we call it? Let's see. . . . How about 'The Ballad of Sam Thayer?' "

Sam groaned self-consciously.

"How about 'The Ballad of Sam Thayer and Company'?" from Irish.

"And how about 'The Ballad of the Women Left Behind to Cook and Wash and Keep the Children from Killing Themselves?' " Maggie smiled wryly.

"Never happen, Ma," said Jamie with a yawn.

"And why not, young sir?"

Johnny answered for his son. "It's not epic enough, Meg."

Maggie glared. "What could be more epic than centuries of women washing and cooking and caring for their men and children, all the while following them to remote corners of the world?"

"Oregon is not that remote!"

Jamie slipped away from the argument to return with the instruments. "I don't care what you play. But we ought to be celebrating something tonight! If nothing else, it stopped raining!"

Johnny picked up the concertina and began to sing, making up the lyrics as he went along: "Ain't gonna rain no more, no more, ain't gonna rain no more. . . ."

Maggie shrugged, laughed, and joined in with the others.

There was plenty of good hard hickory wood for the taking next to the creek, and all during the next pleasant day, the men and children gathered piles of it for future fires, while most of the women sat around mending torn trail clothing and smoking strips of jerky over constant fires.

Maggie had a big soup pot going, cooking up a rich broth from the bones of the elk. On top of her other labors, she'd begged one of the skins. Now the green hide was pegged to the ground, the way her friend Flower Blossom had shown her, and Maggie was carefully scraping from it the last bits of fat preparatory to beginning the long softening process. For that softening, she was boiling the elk's brain in a little water. Flower Blossom had always averred that brain tanning made the softest skins. "Ma-gee," she would point out, "Ma-gee, each animal has enough of the brains to tan itself. The Great Spirit thinks of everything." Maggie smiled as her friend's words returned to her.

Then she shooed Bacon and his sharp little teeth from the irresistible edges of the skin. "Jamie, please convince your pet that he can't play tug-of-war with my pelt! Either that, or lock him up in the wagon. If our boots give out down the trail, we'll need every square inch of this skin for moccasins!"

Jamie had been watching her with interest each time he returned with an armful of wood for their pile. He gathered up the pup obediently, but still seemed anxious about something. As he wrestled with the pup, he finally spit it out. "I know you got moccasins in mind for that skin, Ma, but if, just *if* there should be enough left over. . . ."

"Yes, Jamie?" She smiled at his unusual efforts at beating around the bush.

"Well, Ma, I'd dearly love an elkskin vest, like the kind Straight Arrow and Running Bear used to wear back in Independence, with the rawhide tassels and all. 'Course I'd covet a whole buckskin jacket even more, but I know there won't be enough left for that."

Maggie scrutinized the skin laid out before her. "There surely won't be enough for a jacket, not if we'll be needing moccasins. But there just might be enough for a vest for a very good, smallish boy."

Jamie let out a whoop. "And maybe you could sew on a handful of those Injun beads we brought for trading? We got a whole barrel of 'em!"

Maggie laughed. "I think the Indians could spare a few, Jamie."

He let out another whoop.

"It won't be ready for months, of course. I'll have to soften the skin first, and that takes a long time. There'll be the cutting next, and the fitting and sewing—"

"Maybe by cool weather?"

"I should be able to manage it before autumn."

"Thank you, Ma!" He bounded over to give her a big hug, crushing a yelping Bacon between them. At last he was scampering off for the trees again, Bacon now discarded to nip at his heels and follow.

"Wait'll I tell Matty and Jube! Won't they be wantin' 'em, too!"

Maggie had to chuckle. Now he'd go and start something.

True to her expectations, Hazel headed over from her camp across the large circle of grass between wagons not too many minutes later, her baby in her arms. "Maggie Stuart! What have you got me into? I have no idea how to preserve a hide!"

Maggie glanced up from her work and was relieved to find Hazel smiling. "Jamie works fast. But it's not really hard to learn how, Hazel, just tedious. And it could come in handy. Have Max put in for a skin at the next hunting. The trick is to clean it up quickly and keep it pliant."

Hazel squatted down next to the skin. "How'd you do that?"

"Save some brains or even bone marrow and keep rubbing it in. You make a mix of it with a little moss." Maggie demonstrated as she caked up her elk brains like a bar of lye soap. "Then find a nice palm-sized sandstone, like this one." She flourished the stone she'd chosen for the task. "You keep running it over the skin till it softens up. After I finish cleaning the hide, I'll have Johnny make me a stretcher for it. We can mount it outside the whitetop on dry days and have a go at it now and again."

"How you make everything sound so easy beats me. Max will get me a skin eventually, but I'm bound to mess it up."

"You need to have more faith in yourself, Hazel." Maggie eased back from her tiring task to stretch her shoulders and pick up Charlotte from the corral next to her. Then the two women began to companionably nurse their daughters. "The way I look at it, you'll never know how hard or easy a task is until you set your mind to it. If you stop worrying and just lay into it, it will come out better than you thought. And it's the only way to learn."

Hazel accepted her words as they sat watching the bustling scene around them. Grandma Richman must have done another load of washing, for she was trying to drape an armful of wet laundry over her wagon while chasing two grandchildren away from their family fire. Ruth Winslow had a Bible spread open on her wagon tongue, and kept going between it and her own fire with a frown of concentration on her face. The Peterson and Jarboe and Simpson women were working on dinner, and Josh Chandler's wife and elder daughters were busy stitching.

Hazel followed Maggie's eyes. "Gwen don't seem to be around. She off scrounging for wood with the men?"

"Could be. Then again, maybe she's walking with Sam Thayer."

"Sam Thayer?" Hazel's eyes widened with anticipation. "You don't suppose. . . ."

Maggie grinned. "I did happen to spot Sam, hat in hand, shyly approach the Hardisty wagon earlier this morning."

"Sam couldn't be courting Gwen, could he? In his own good time and way?"

Maggie allowed her mind to speed ahead with the

idea. "Sam's about thirty-five, Hazel, the perfect age for Gwen."

"He's a good, solid, steady man, too, Maggie. And neither of them too old yet to be starting a family."

Maggie laughed out loud. "Indeed. All in all, it could be a most satisfactory arrangement." It was also one most pleasing to her sense of fitness and romance. Since she was so happy with her own husband, she felt that everyone should have the same opportunity to be cherished and loved. Enjoying the idea more and more, Maggie sat with Hazel beaming over it, thoroughly content with the day.

Eventually the babies finished their nursing, and Hazel wandered back to her own camp to tend her midday meal. Maggie strapped Charlotte to her back, slung her gathering bag around her shoulder, and went in search of something green to throw in her soup pot.

After all the rains, the glorious weather was most welcome. And it was a pleasure to be wandering almost for the sake of it, rather than eternally beside her teams of recalcitrant oxen.

Maggie lifted her eyes to watch the stock grazing placidly on the verdant grass around the outer limits of the camp, loosely guarded by the camp's older boys. The grass just seemed to go on forever, off into the prairie horizon, green blending into a sea of sky blue. Bees hovered over blossoms and quick, darting birds dove for insects.

Maggie knelt to study a vividly colored butterfly as it feasted on a dandelion blossom. Unthinking, she held out her hand and it flew to her. Charlotte reached over her mother's shoulder to grab at the resting bit of orange and yellow loveliness. The butterfly fluttered its wings and took flight once more. Maggie followed its arc.

"It seems perfect, daughter. Everything is perfect, just as God made it." She felt very close to Him this morning as Charlotte crowed her delighted agreement.

The day of rest passed with tranquility. And when they rose in the morning to cross the Big Vermillion, humans and stock alike went at it with new enthusiasm.

nine

Two days later, under a still-smiling sky, the Chandler Party paused for nooning at an unusual rock formation that jutted from the east bank of the Big Blue River. There was rumored to be a spring of clear, cool water nearby and a waterfall of some twelve feet, surrounded by a little grove of cottonwood and cedar trees.

When Maggie searched for Jamie to collect wood, she found him already gone. Maggie unstrapped the baby from her back, tucked her into the cabin for a nap, and went off to collect branches herself. Soon she heard the whoops of laughing children.

Following the sounds, she came upon the falls, first tripping on a pile of hastily discarded clothing. Her missing son—and most of the other boys—were buck naked, playing tag under the cascading water.

Maggie grinned at their delight, wishing she could discard her own skirts and join in the fun. It was a joy to watch the youngsters become carefree again for a brief time, stripped of their chores as well as their raiment.

She was stretching out her hand to dip a handkerchief into the cool water to wash her own face when a strong, strident step sounded behind her. It was the Reverend Winslow, with a freshly cut switch in hand and a thunderous expression upon his face. What now? Hadn't he seen children frolicking before?

"Jedediah Winslow!" he roared. "Get thee hither!

107

Also Jonah, Job, and Jeremiah!"

Four skinny boys emerged from the water, crest-fallen.

The eldest dared to speak. "But Father, we were doing no harm. We hardly spoke to the others, and certainly nothing about—"

Before he could finish, the switch was cracked across the oldest boy's buttocks, five times. Purple with rage, the Reverend Winslow lowered his stick to point mutely at the pile of clothing. The other three boys stood in line patiently, awaiting their own punishment.

Maggie watched with horror, too surprised by the action to respond until Winslow worked his way to the smallest, not more than four years old. Helpless to do anything else, she put out her arms in an attempt to save the trembling child.

"Out of my way, woman, lest I strike thee as well in my just fury!"

Maggie would not be budged as the little boy shivered in her embrace. An ominous silence descended in the grove as the children remaining beneath the waterfall ceased their game and stared with fright.

"What has caused your just fury, Reverend Winslow? The children are only bathing, refreshing themselves from the heat of the trail."

His stick remained raised. "My sons have their traveling orders. They have disobeyed their father, thus broken one of the Ten Commandments."

"Aren't you interpreting 'Honor thy father' too harshly?"

"You'll not be telling me how to interpret the Scripture! But if the Commandments are not enough to satisfy you, we may move on to the Prophet Isaiah: 'When you see the naked, clothe them.' "

Maggie still held on to the youngest. "But the Bible also says, 'Naked came I out of my mother's womb, and naked shall I return.' There is nothing wicked in nakedness, certainly not among innocent children. Is it not better 'to clothe oneself with compassion, kindness, humility, gentleness, and patience'?"

"You misconstrue and misquote the Lord's Word. Such defilement makes you no better than the Mormons, who attempt to force new scriptural *revelations* on the world. Get thee from me, Satan!"

Winslow, brimstone in his eyes, hauled the youngest from Maggie's grasp and lowered his switch. The smallest boy hadn't yet learned the stoicism of his elder brothers. With each strike, he let out howls of anguish. The stick came down five times, then an added sixth. "To chase out the devil," Winslow explained briefly to Maggie before stalking off.

Maggie stared after the departing figure before turning to the little boy. She gathered him into her arms once more and let him finish crying in comfort against her bosom. Then she wiped the blazing welts on his bottom with icy water and helped him into his britches.

When she sent Jeremiah Winslow off, she found Jamie by her side, already pulling on his own pants. "Don't you want to finish playing, son?"

Jamie gave her a wet hug. "It's kind of spoiled now, Ma. You understand?"

"Yes, I think I do."

Jamie gazed through the trees at the wagons beyond, then gave her another hug.

Maggie smiled. "And what was that one for?"

"He could of 'dopted me, instead of you and Pa."

Maggie saw the seriousness in her son's eyes. "But he didn't. Now get into the rest of your clothes and find some more wood for the campfire. It's almost time to eat."

Word of the confrontation between Maggie and Winslow had spread quickly through the camp. Maggie saw a few awed looks directed toward her as she walked back. Johnny just gave her a very firm kiss and continued to empty the stale water from their barrels preparatory to refilling them with cool, fresh water from the spring.

Less than half a mile from the spring, they came to the Independence Crossing of the Big Blue. It was still high from the rains and would permit an unpredictable fording at best. The emigrants studied the stream's rapid current and gravelly bottom for some minutes.

Finally, Sam walked up to the Stuarts. "Gonna have to raise the wagon beds some to get over dry."

Johnny gave Sam his full attention. "What do you think is the best way?"

"Have to place some blocks between the beds and the bolsters, then lower the wagons down with ropes like at the Kansas crossing."

Johnny turned from his assessment of the water. "Let's get started, then, Sam."

Maggie estimated that they averaged about five wagons an hour in the crossing. They got over dry, but that was all they managed to do for the rest of that day. It was far into the night before the final wagon had made it.

They'd pulled lots for the crossing order, Chandler reasoning it was the most democratic way to get the job done. Everyone had to remember their numbers, too, and each family would move up to the front of the line, one wagon at a time, for future crossings. The Stuarts had pulled number fifteen, almost dead center, so it would be a while before they made it to the head of the train.

Chandler also decided that they'd travel in their lot orders between crossings for the present. It wouldn't make that much difference now, while the prairie was still moist, but it could make a big difference come dryness and dust on the trail. Then they'd move up one wagon each day. This rotation would keep the slower of them from coughing up all the dust made by the leading white-tops.

Fine weather brought the emigrants outdoors at night, too, rolled up in blankets or beneath tents which began to spring up within the circled corral of wagons.

The night of the Big Blue crossing, Johnny and Maggie bunked the children down in the book wagon and took to the open air themselves, beneath a little tent that Johnny had raised for privacy. Mos-

quitoes hadn't yet appeared, and they lay next to
each other, relishing the quiet and the rare chance to
be together, alone.

Johnny finally got around to the nooning incident.
"What did you do to Winslow today? He's been
giving all of us the blackest looks. Especially since
his youngest wandered over here during supper to
moon over you."

"Little Jeremiah? Poor thing. He had to do some
wandering. I doubt he'll be able to sit for a week
with the thrashing his father gave him."

"You're evading the point, my love."

Maggie snuggled closer to her husband. "I just
gave him a taste of his own medicine. I quoted the
Bible back at him after he half-killed three of his
sons. I was trying to save the little one, but only
made it worse. Winslow said I was 'worse than the
Mormons,' thrashed the boy harder, and stomped
off."

Johnny gently ran his hands over her face, mull-
ing over her words.

"What is this hatred Winslow has of the Mormons, Johnny? He's like Bacon chewing at a bone.
And those instructions he's given his family not to
talk to any of the rest of the party? It's unnatural, as
if he's trying to hide some awful secret."

Johnny did not hazard an opinion, but asked a
question of his own. "What were you telling me
about that little talk you had with his wife the other
day?"

"She was frightened . . . said something about
Illinois."

"There was another word you mentioned, Meg. I think it's the key. *Mormons*. *Mormons* and *Illinois*." Johnny flopped over onto his back to concentrate.

Suddenly, he shot upright in the low tent, almost knocking it down. His words came out intensely, in his Eureka! voice. "That's it, Meg! I'll bet you anything the family's originally from Illinois, and probably one of the towns near Nauvoo, too. Carthage or Quincy, maybe. Nice little towns they were. Remember going through them after Charley was born?" He didn't wait for her answer. "No, you wouldn't. You were far too exhausted from the birthing. Wasn't it in Carthage that the Mormons' leader, Joseph Smith, was shot?"

Johnny slowly settled back down again to face her. "If that's the case, and he's still got Mormons on his mind. . . . I wonder what Winslow was really up to back there?"

"Why don't you ask the man, Johnny?"

"After your experience today?" He laughed, but quickly sobered. "Winslow's a hard enemy to have. Already he's drumming up opposition to Chandler's leadership."

"Why? Chandler seems to be doing the best possible under the circumstances. He hasn't led us wrong yet."

"Life is a search after power, Meg. Some men can't seem to live without it. Winslow's one of them. It's not enough for him to feel absolutely correct. He needs to know that others follow in his compunctions. He wants to lead the train by his own rules. He's been agitating to lay over each Sunday for prayer."

"Well, that's one sentiment we share. It *would* be nice to have a regular day of rest, and some time to give the Lord His due."

"It would also be nice to make it to the mountains before the snows fall and our provisions give out. I've nothing against giving the Lord His due, but He's the One Who keeps the days and weeks and seasons turning. We can't stop that. If we don't make our crossing in the time allotted, we stand a chance of dying in the mountains. I can't see how that would be a help to anyone."

Johnny eased Maggie into his arms and held her close. "Enough of the villain. If Winslow comes near you again, yell for me. I'll always drop everything for you, Meg. You know that. You are dearer to me than all that I possess."

"Even your precious printing press?" she teased.

But his next words were delivered earnestly, with no hint of levity. "You're the inspiration for the words that shall come forth from that press."

ten

"Maggie!"

At Johnny's rough shake, she bolted from her blankets. "What is it? Morning already?"

"Indians again. They ran off with half a dozen horses last night—one of them Max's prize stallion, and two of Chandler's blooded Morgan mares."

A hand reached for her skirt. "But we had sentries posted!"

Johnny was grim. "One. Hal Richman pulled the lot. And came back for his jug after the camp was quiet. They found him dead drunk in the grass just outside the wagons, and the horses carefully picked out. Got to hand it to them, Indians know their horseflesh, even in the dark!"

Maggie was already fastening her buttons. "Do you think it was the Caws we met?"

"Nobody's sure. But we're getting closer to the Platte. Pawnee country. And Pawnees wander farther afield than most tribes."

"They're not even half-civilized, are they?" Meg could not hide her concern.

"Not the last I heard."

"At least they spared Dickens and Miss Sally."

Johnny gave a harsh laugh. "Those two are not precisely prime horseflesh. They're dray animals. Indians look for good breeders, fast ones. But if they're allowed to pick off the others, even Miss

Sally may become tempting."

"What will we do?"

"For starters, post two sentries from now on, and maybe split shifts halfway through the night with another two. Chandler can't miss the wisdom of that. And maybe if we're very lucky, the thieves will bring the horses back for trade." He slowly inched out of the small tent.

"Where are you going, Johnny?" Maggie was getting that prickly Indian feeling again and was loath to have her husband out of her sight.

"To have a powwow with Chandler. Something's got to be done about that Richman anyway. The man's incompetent enough without the drink!"

"Try to be charitable, Johnny. He's still mourning his wife."

"A real man doesn't mourn with a jug of rum! My own father swallowed enough of it in his day, and it may have weakened his knees, but never his mind!"

They were several hours on the trail when a low buzz moved through the train. Maggie made out riders coming at them from the south. It was a band of Indians, what tribe she couldn't even guess. And trailing behind them was a string of horses! Was it possible? Could they be returning the stolen stock?

The lead wagon came to a halt and obediently the others followed. There was going to be a negotiation session. Johnny halted his wagon in front of Maggie and dashed to the back to pull out his rifle. He'd stopped keeping it in the book wagon after the first Indian incident.

Maggie, her back already aching from Charlotte's weight, pulled the baby out of her harness and caught her husband before he disappeared.

She nodded toward the Indians closing in on them. "What do you think?"

"I'm thinking thieving Pawnee. They've got feathers in their hair, different from the Caw. The one at the front—he's got a full headdress of them—looks a lot like that lithograph of Petalesharo who went to visit 'The Great White Father' in Washington back in the 'twenties. Stick close to both wagons, Meg. They'll be swarming over us in a minute, and there's no telling what else they'll try to steal."

Jamie ran up, already begging. "May I go with you, Pa, please?"

For once, Johnny was adamant. "Absolutely not. We don't know what we're dealing with here. You help your mother. Shoo away anyone who comes near." Johnny cracked his rifle to load it. "Close work like this, I almost wish I had a brace of pistols."

"You wouldn't actually shoot at them, would you, Johnny?"

He sighed. "I know they're human beings, Meg, more than most here. I know they figure we're trespassing on their property, using up their grass and water. They're more than half-right. I'd surely hate to injure any man, Indian or not. But it's my job to protect my family—and if it comes to that, I'll do my duty!"

Jamie was gaping at his father in adulation. Maggie only shuddered as she watched her husband stride purposefully away. Unthinking, she voiced her thoughts aloud. "Why must we be in conflict with the Indians? Can't we just pass through and leave each other undisturbed?"

"Awful hard to keep the Injuns undisturbed, Ma. Seems like we've been disturbing them farther west since white folks first got to America."

She shot a sharp glance at her son. She sometimes forgot the wisdom of a seven-year-old—at least, this seven-year-old. "Where have you found such thoughts, Jamie?"

He shrugged. "Just paging through my *McGuffey's* and some of Pa's other books. Did you know that Squanto, the one who helped the Pilgrims, was kidnapped off to England two or three times? And Pocahantas—"

"Those Indians are long dead, son. Don't these real, live ones frighten you?"

"Nope. They're kind of interesting, though. Before we left Independence, thought I'd never see an untamed kind. Straight Arrow and Running Bear and their ma, well, they were pretty close to civilized by the time we left. These wild ones dress pretty, don't they? Kind of like birds or animals." He waved off toward the grouping in the distance. "Take that one getting off his horse, Ma. His leather pants are all painted with decorations. Wouldn't it be nice to own a pair of britches like that!"

Maggie followed her son's gaze. Jamie was right

about the Pawnees' dress and bearing. These Indians had a natural grace and beauty. They also had an insolence rarely seen in the Indians parading the streets of Independence. These braves had not been dispossessed. Maggie shook her head. She also suspected that all those horizontal stripes on the leggings stood for something dreadful, like the number of scalps taken in battle.

The intruders closed in on the camp. Maggie followed their movements. They were not exactly hostile—rather, sly. Would there be Indians like this in the Territory? Would she be comfortable in teaching them alongside Johnny? Surely they wouldn't have such a savage, ferocious demeanor.

Maggie clung to her baby, one arm stretched out to grasp Jamie's shoulder sharply. The Indians were coming nearer. Dismounting completed, the leader with the headdress stood aside to talk with Chandler and the group of emigrant men surrounding him. Smoothly, almost unobtrusively, the other braves were dispersing down the line, pausing here or there to remark upon something to each other with a guttural grunt or laugh.

Before Maggie could think, a brave was before her, poking his head into the back of Johnny's white-top, coming to rest against the book wagon next to her, his fingers touching the fading flowers and animals she'd painted on the side.

Then he was boldly confronting Maggie and her children, smelling different from any man she'd ever met. It was a strong smell, of animal grease and dirt and something else—something feral.

Maggie broke out in a cold sweat as the brave's hand was raised first to Charlotte's red head, then to her own.

She must not show fear. He probably meant her no harm. His knife was sheathed, his rifle pointed down. But the touch brought Gwen's words about men back to her. Especially the dread of being touched. At this moment, Maggie was petrified by the Indian's touch.

Jamie, however, was fascinated. He stared at the bronzed man as brazenly as the Indian was staring at them. Finally, Jamie broke away from Maggie to tug at the Indian's arm. The Indian looked down, an expression close to amusement in his eyes.

"Excuse me, sir, but I powerfully admire your britches. That's a fine snake slithering down your one leg. And is that horse hair, all braided up like that? Or," he added hopefully, "maybe human hair?"

Maggie moved swiftly, unconsciously, to pull her son back within her grasp.

The Indian laughed, then made an obvious eating motion, fingers held to his mouth like a scoop.

Maggie loosed her son again. "Jamie? Run into the wagon. Grab a hunk of bacon. Bring it out."

Jamie caught the tension in his mother's voice and obeyed without question, forgetting the other things he wanted to ask the fascinating wild Indian.

Maggie kept her own eyes locked on the brave's until the boy returned. She mustn't allow the Indian into their wagon. That much she understood. This was not Independence, and he was not Black Raven. This situation had nothing to do with being a neighborly Christian. It was more on the order of highway robbery. If she could only keep his attention. . . .

Jamie finally appeared, hands laden with food. Following him was Bacon, shaking the sleep from his puppy body. For one brief second, the little coyote took in the Indian's sight and smell before a strange conversion overtook him. He raised his hackles, bared his teeth. Then he raced ahead of Jamie and lunged at the Pawnee's leg. His baby teeth could do small harm, but the animal bit in and clung ferociously.

The brave finally broke his eye contact with Maggie, shook the pup off his leg, and calmly but methodically gave it a vicious kick. Bacon sprawled on the ground, shocked, before gamely picking himself up for a second attack. The Indian unsheathed his knife and held it at the ready.

"No! No! Please don't hurt my dog!" Jamie shoved the meat at the man and ran to gather up Bacon. The animal tried to free himself of his friend's protection, actually giving Jamie a good scratch with his nails, but suddenly whimpered and flopped back against the boy.

"Take Bacon into the wagon, Jamie. Stay with him. I'll check how badly he's hurt as soon as our visitor leaves."

All this time Maggie never allowed her eyes to wander from the intruder. Now she gave him a look of pure, unbridled anger and contempt. It was understandable in any language. The Indian slowly sheathed his knife. He gave her a final glare of his own, bent to pick up the bacon that had fallen, and stalked off.

Maggie exhaled slowly. She dropped her squirming child to lean against the wagon, gasping in lungfuls of air. Still shaking, she managed finally to bend over to examine the undersides of both wagons, walking their circumference, to make sure there were no unexpected loiterers left to surprise her. Only after she'd caught up with the crawling Charlotte—almost under the oxen's feet—did she turn to the meeting place up ahead.

An understanding must have been reached. The stolen horses were now in the hands of the emigrants, and the Indians were gathered again, carefully packing bolts of cloth and other commodities onto their own animals.

Johnny was grim-faced when he returned. "We're packing the stock inside the circle of wagons tonight. They won't have as much grazing possibilities, but we daren't take another chance with these villainous bandits so close."

"What did they say, Johnny?"

He rubbed his forehead wearily. "Said they'd *found* the animals wandering loose. They were just returning them to oblige us. It cost the owners a fair penny, it did, this little incident."

He went to the water bag hanging from outside the book wagon and ladled a scoop over his head before drinking deeply. He finally inspected his wife. "What happened here? You've lost a week's worth of sun from your face."

Maggie took the water scoop from his hand and

helped herself to a drink. She gagged on it. "We had our own little encounter. One of the men stopped here. He seemed fascinated by my hair, and the baby's. He wouldn't leave. Then Bacon woke up and attacked him. . . . Oh, Johnny!"

Johnny took Charlotte from her arms and tried to gather in Maggie, too.

"I don't think he took anything aside from the meat we gave him, but he did frighten me so!"

Johnny ran his free hand down her cheek, trying to calm her. "Jamie and the pup. Are they all right?"

"I don't know. Bacon may be injured. The brute gave him a ferocious kick, and the little thing just whimpered and finally gave up."

"Let's go find out."

Inside the wagon, Jamie was curled up in the bottom bunk, humming tunelessly to the coyote. Johnny sat down and carefully picked up the pup, fingers feeling gently for ribs beginning to flesh out.

Finally he set the animal down again. "Let him rest, Jamie. Nothing seems broken. He may just be bruised a little, in spirit, too. He took on a big job trying to protect you. He probably feels he let you down."

"Bacon couldn't ever do that! It's all right, Bacon. You did a good job. That old Injun can keep his fancy pants. Didn't really like 'em anyway." The crooning began again.

Johnny smiled at Maggie. "Maybe Jamie would like to ride with Bacon and Charlotte for a piece.

I'll keep an eye on them both, and give you a little breathing space."

Jamie stopped midnote. "I'll stay, Pa, till Ma needs me."

Outside, Johnny quietly held his wife. "Wish I could walk with you. You'll be all right?"

Maggie was loath to let him go, but finally did. "The McDonalds didn't breed any shirkers, Johnny. I'll manage. But I'm not looking forward to any more wild Indians!"

eleven

The week following the Pawnee horse exchange passed with little incident. The travelers stepped up their security and made good time on the drying prairie. In fact, they sometimes covered more than twelve miles a day by their best estimates, figuring from the sparse sites given in the few guidebooks in the train's possession. An occasional Indian band— the same Pawnee or perhaps different ones entirely, they were never completely sure—was seen at a distance, outlined against the horizon.

Once they were stopped at a minor stream and pressed for toll by a handful of Kickapoo. Grumbling inwardly at the blackmail, the men followed Chandler's lead, paying out the twenty-five cents per wagon demanded.

Maggie didn't mind either the Kickapoo or their requested toll, for the braves straddling their mounts around the shallow creek had none of the insolence or self-possession of the Pawnee. Their apparel was a motley assortment of Indian skins and trade blankets, and one rather venerable-looking old fellow was holding onto a Christian prayer stick in lieu of a rifle.

Her heart went out to them in their obvious confusion and weariness. They'd lost the will to plunder as though it were their right—like the Pawnee. These Kickapoo had become just another tribe caught between two worlds.

She dared not share these most private thoughts with anyone but Johnny. Sentiment against the Indians had begun to grow and fester, along with the fear of what could actually happen should the red men be crossed. Now it was no longer the Mormons who provided the primary topic for their fireside discussions.

On the seventh night after the horse exchange, Max walked over during dinner and handed Maggie a small parcel. "Hazel sent some butter. It churned up nice for her in the wagon this afternoon."

Maggie smiled. "It'll taste good on the fry bread. Thank Hazel for me." She nodded at the pot. "Care for some beans, Max? We've got plenty."

"I just ate, but might be room for a spoonful. That ain't why I came, though."

Sam put down his plate. "Spit it out."

Max was not eager to spit it out. He accepted his beans first, carefully tasting them before choosing his words. "Down by the stream. Tracks were left in the mud from last night's storm. Horses, mostly unshod. Not ours. And footprints, too. Moccasins. Could be the band we spotted off in the distance just before noon."

Irish blurted out an oath. Then he shrugged an apology to the ladies. "Sorry. But I've got sentry duty tonight. The midnight shift. With Richman! Wouldn't you know I'd pull duty with him when there was a real chance of Indians around!"

"Just don't let him get near his jug, Irish."

Irish grinned ruefully at Johnny. "You can bet I won't! Won't let him near the wagons at all. But he'd better keep his distance from me."

"Is it fair to keep treating the man like a pariah?" Maggie looked at Max. "I know he's already cost you dearly, but you did get your stallion back, and we all learned from the experience. He taught us a necessary lesson, and perhaps in good time."

Max finished his beans and reached for his pipe. "I'm doing my Christian best to put all that behind me. Others been a little less forgiving, though. Winslow got back his horses, too, but never goes by the man without giving him a temperance lecture. If I was Richman, that alone would be enough to drive me to drink harder."

Maggie threw more batter into her pan and carefully handed Jamie some finished bread with a dab of butter on top. The boy immediately broke it in two and shared half with the waiting coyote.

"Save the butter for yourself, son. I'm not sure it's good for the pup's digestion." She turned back to the adults. "I don't suppose there's anything to be done about the Reverend Winslow? He tends to cast a shadow over everyone's daily affairs."

Gwen smiled. "You have such a pretty way of putting things, Maggie. He stopped by our wagon today to castigate me for causing last night's thunderstorm."

Sam scowled. "Didn't mention naught to me about that, Gwen."

Gwen colored. "I didn't want to upset you, Sam."

"What exactly did he say?"

"I was, well. . . . You know how hot it got about midday. I was tucking up my skirts for some air . . .

not more than an inch or two above the ankles, it was." She paused to blush again. "The man walked by just then—"

"Why wasn't he tendin' his own wagon!"

"Well, you know how he leaves it for his wife and goes poking about."

"What did he say, Gwen!"

"Oh, Sam." She looked pointedly at Jamie.

Johnny spoke up. "Son, if you're finished with your dinner, why don't you take Bacon for his evening constitutional."

"May I go see how Jube's doing?"

"Fine. But don't be too long."

With Jamie's departure, attention turned to the flustered Gwen.

"I never meant to bring this up at all," she wailed.

"It's all right, Gwen." Johnny's tone was comforting. "He's been at my wife, too. It might help us to figure out what's troubling the man."

"Everything's troubling him!" let out Gwen in a sudden rush. "The heathens, the non-existent Mormons, the way I wear my hair, the storms. For a man of God, he's the most troubled person I've ever met! He called me 'the harlot of Babylon' today. Said I was enticing fine married men with my loose ways, bringing God's wrath down upon us all! He said I'd better watch out for the Indians, too, since they'd taken to the Mormons' practice of having extra wives—"

Gwen's vehemence petered out, and it looked fairly questionable as to whether she'd laugh or cry next. Her heightened emotions only emphasized her coloring, however, gave strength to her face, and made her more attractive than ever.

Maggie glanced at Sam. The veins on his neck were standing out, and his face had become as thunderous as the heavens the previous night. She was afraid he might erupt.

Luckily, Johnny had noticed, too. He reached over to give his big friend a hearty slap on the back. "What would that make Grandma Richman, Sam? She had her skirts hiked up to her knees today, showing off some very handsome petticoats. I even spotted some lace! Think the Indians—or Mormons—will want to take her on, too?"

Sam calmed down with the round of chuckles. But he inched closer to Gwen, tentatively reaching out his hand to touch hers. Maggie watched with bated breath. Would the gesture be accepted? She could almost read the sudden confusion in Gwen's face. Hesitantly, her hand stretched to meet Sam's. Maggie almost sighed audibly, while Johnny filled in the silence.

"I always wondered how women coped with all those skirts. I've heard that some on far-out spreads even take to wearing their husbands' pants." His eyes gleamed at Maggie, and he reached his own hand out for hers. "I can't say that I wouldn't be curious to see the effect."

"On one, Johnny. I trust you really mean on one." They both laughed as she accepted his hand.

Max rose. "Better get back to help tuck the girls in."

Irish joined him. "Better tuck myself in. Midnight

will come sooner than I'd like, and that's for sure."
He paused a moment, looking up at the night sky.
"Still, there might be a moment to mosey over to
pay my respects to the Chandlers. Just to see how
they're holding up under the latest news."

Maggie chuckled as she watched Irish make a
beeline for the charms of young Susan Chandler,
then leaned closer to Johnny as Sam pulled Gwen up
for a walk. Adversity did create some positive re-
sults. Irish was showing signs of becoming a serious
suitor to Chandler's daughter, and there was a warm
friendship budding between Gwen and Sam. If Sam
had his way, and weren't too forward. . . .

"There's matchmaking in your eyes, my girl. I've
seen it before."

"And why not?"

Johnny put his arm around his wife. "Why not,
indeed. Were all couples as well-matched as ourselves, there'd be considerable less strife in the
world."

He bent his head to whisper something into her
ear. She blushed, but drew closer. It was dark now,
and their forms were outlined by the dimming light
of their fire. Johnny glanced around once, then
swung Meg low, and gave her a dramatic kiss.

"Your son is still wandering around out there,"
Maggie protested feebly.

"Ah, now he's *my* son!"

"You wouldn't want him to—" Johnny was nib-
bling at her ear.

"Want him to what? See us kissing? It will do him
good to know that his parents have a yen for each

other. Or do you think he'll run off to tattle to the Reverend?"

Maggie laughed and sat up. "Unlikely. But get him, please. I'll feel better when he's where I know he's safe. You never can tell who's prowling around outside the wagons." She trembled at the thought. Johnny immediately understood, she knew, as he understood all things about her.

"I'll get him. But don't you be doing any wandering! I'm coming back to finish what I started."

"I'll be waiting, Johnny!"

Irish was awakened by Jed Smith; he'd been having a strange dream. He'd made the Territory and found a pit of the highest quality clay right out beyond his cabin. Anxious to start work, he'd hauled out his wheel, but instead of throwing pots, he found himself creating vast, life-size sculptures of animals—elk, bear, buffalo. Huge clay forms surrounded him, but he could not quite complete any of them. He sat scratching his head, deep in a conundrum. He wanted his animals perfect, and they were, but for one thing. He looked at the bear. Did it have a navel? What about the buffalo, the horse? Did animals have belly buttons? He was shaken again, more roughly.

"It's midnight, Hardisty, your shift!" The voice was a harsh whisper.

Irish rolled over and up and in a minute was outside his small tent, blinking. He grabbed at Jed Smith as he turned wearily to leave. "Those elk we bagged . . . did they have belly buttons?"

Smith's face was inscrutable in the darkness. "You been at the jug, too, Hardisty?"

Irish shook his head. "Never mind. Just a dream. I'm up now."

"Where's your rifle?"

"Oh." Irish grinned charmingly, but it was lost to the night and Smith's receding figure. He bent for the rifle and slipped between the wagons, out of the circle of security, into the vastness of the plains and its mysteries.

Johnny and Maggie were still asleep when the shot rang out. Johnny sprang up, instantly alert.

Maggie reached for him, to draw him close again. "What is it, Johnny?" Her voice was soft and sleep-logged.

"Trouble." He pulled on his pants and boots, grabbed his shirt, and sprang out of the tent, toward the sound that was still echoing in his mind. A second later he was back, reaching for the rifle that now went everywhere with him.

"Should I—" Her voice trailed off.

"Stay. Sleep. I'll be back."

There were no further shots, but slowly the camp came to life. The pre-dawn stillness was lit with lanterns, small will-o'-the-wisps flitting between wagons, hushed tones following them in an effort to keep the young ones asleep. Johnny had come back from the prairie with Irish in tow, tears streaming down the potter's youthful face. Next had come several half-dressed men hauling a body between them.

After tossing restlessly in Johnny's absence for several minutes, Maggie sensed something was very wrong. She dressed as quickly as possible and went out to learn what had happened.

Hal Richman was spread out on the ground near a low fire. There was a bloody cavity where his chest used to be. Maggie took in the shocked expressions in the circle surrounding the man, then quickly stooped down to touch him.

"He's still alive! What happened?" She searched for an answer from the stricken faces. "Never mind what happened. Where's Grandma? And how about some cloth? We've got to stop the blood!"

Not waiting to see what was being done, Maggie slipped off the petticoat she'd only just gotten into and began stripping it into pieces.

"Somebody give me a knife, *please*!"

The crowd came alive, and she grabbed at an offered knife, using it to rip off Richman's shirt and tear away his longjohns. His chest looked bad. She wadded up some of the cloth and shoved it into the wound, putting pressure on the area. Finally, Grandma appeared, took one look and took over.

Maggie rose. Irish was sitting on an upturned box in the darkness beyond the fire, stricken. Johnny was crouched next to him, with a supporting hand on his shoulder.

She walked over. "Is someone ready to explain?"

Johnny sighed. "Richman rose out of the grass, shrouded in a blanket like an Indian. Irish called out, but Richman didn't answer. So Irish shot him."

"Father God, help us all." Maggie's soft words

were both prayer and testimony to her utter help-
lessness. Her knees buckled and she sank down
upon the damp ground. "It was the footprints. The
Indian talk."

Irish put his face in his hands, and Maggie
reached out to touch him. "It could have been an
Indian, Irish. We know they're out there, following
us." She shoved her mass of loosened hair away
from her face. "I didn't realize you were such a
good shot."

Irish groaned. "He wasn't more than twenty feet
away. I could hardly have missed. It was so dark, the
moon already set, but the blanket . . . and he seemed
to have a feather in his hair."

"It was only a twig sticking up." Maggie sighed.
"I pulled it out of his hair just now. He was sleeping
on duty again, and had probably just woken. He was
drinking, too. His breath was strong. I'd guess he
didn't even see you."

She paused. The deed could not be undone. The
finality of it was frightening. "At least I don't think
he's feeling any pain. Pray God he's not."

There was a low murmur from where Richman
lay, and Sam and Max slowly walked to them.

Irish raised his head from his hands. "Is he dead?"

Max nodded and Irish slumped into Johnny. "God
forgive me. He had *eight* children!"

"And not an ounce of sense in his head." It was
Sam speaking. "He was given a trust, and he let all
of us down. You're not to be blamed, Hardisty. I
would have taken the shot myself."

The other men nodded as Gwen came bustling up,

slightly late and out of breath, slightly out of touch, as usual. She took in the tableau before her, her hands slowly falling from the golden plaits she was working. Sam came to put a bearlike arm around her, to draw her protectively to himself, and the story was retold again.

They buried Hal Richman with his jug. The grave was started at first light, before the day's heat could do further damage to his body. Grandma Richman supervised, brushing an occasional tear from her eye, an occasional youngster out of the way of progress.

"Set him out straight, now. That's right. Asa! Fetch your Daddy's best shirt, and his spare jug. Musta lost the other one in the grass last night."

Asa dutifully returned, and Grandma jumped into the shallow grave and dressed her son for the last time. She set the almost-full jug lovingly next to his body and draped his raising arm around it. Her eyes made one final survey, seeing that all was as well as it could be before hauling herself up again.

Grandma peered through her spectacles at the full complement of the train surrounding her. "Know you don't approve of me buryin' my boy with his jug. It was his folly and his downfall. But it looks right with him there, and with the Good Lord's help, I'm gettin' my grandchildren to the Territory without it!"

Grandma was in charge, and no one, not even Josiah Winslow, was about to cross her. Raising a deep breath from her ample chest, she continued her directions with authority. "Josh Chandler, you're the captain. Duty sets on you to say a few words over 'im."

Her eyes traveled farther around the circle of people. "Reverend Winslow, know you had no truck with my boy, but bein' you're the only clergyman present, I'll thank you to follow up Chandler with a Christian prayer."

Josh Chandler stepped forward from the hushed group. He pulled a huge handkerchief out of his pocket and wiped his forehead with it, then tucked it away. He motioned to smooth out his great, black, chest-length beard, but thought better of it, cleared his throat, and began.

"Friends, we gather here this morning to lay to rest one of our brothers. He weren't a brother by kin, and he weren't even a brother to most of us in friendship." Chandler coughed and spat through thickly mustachioed lips off to the side. "He were, however, a brother in folly and tribulation, which all of us gets mixed up in from time to time. Through his faults, I figure he taught us all a few good lessons, lessons we can all learn by.

"Hal Richman signed a pact with all of us way back outside of Independence. He leaves us his mother, surely stronger in wisdom, and his eight little ones. We all signed that pact together, and I want you all to know that we'll stand by it, and see that his family makes it to where he was plannin' on takin' them!"

Chandler looked around to make sure his words were understood. Pulling out his handkerchief again, he wiped his sweaty hands and stepped back from the grave, giving a nod to Winslow.

There was a little flurry of anticipation amongst the emigrants as Winslow stepped forward. He'd been begging to be given the chance to preach, and now he finally had his opportunity. Some of the smaller children scurried to hide behind their mother's skirts at the sight of the dour, black-coated man, frightened by earlier crossings of his path.

Maggie, with Johnny beside her, glanced quickly around the group. Winslow's wife Ruth was standing straighter than usual, proud that her husband was finally to be where he shone, where he belonged.

Winslow himself had apparently anticipated the occasion. He was clean-shaven and had donned, besides his black frock coat, a fresh, soft shirt and black cravat. He stood gazing down at Hal Richman for a long moment, gathering the attention of the crowd, playing on his audience. Finally he spoke, and the words came out like thunder under the growing heat of the morning sun.

" 'Thy shoes shall be as iron and brass!' " He paused to allow the words to sink in. "Yes, 'Thy shoes shall be as iron and brass!' This text from Deuteronomy must guide us. We must be shod in iron to kick the enemies from under our feet, the heathen Brother Richman was mistaken for, the same heathen that I go to guide into the path of Peace, Understanding, and Faith. We must make level the paths west with our boots! We must keep these feet from slipping, from being weighed down

with dissipation, in *drink*, as this man's feet were
led: in debauchery, lust, and drunkenness!"

He spun around, his eyes directed dangerously
near where the Stuarts stood. "Yes, beneath, and
even outside of our tents at night, such abomina-
tions are practiced, practiced by those who call
themselves Christians! But are we Christians or
Mormons? Mormons call themselves to the flesh;
Christians to God. It is time to stand up and be
counted, lest the Lord forsake us completely in this
Wilderness! He has given us a sign, through our
brother Richman. We must take heed before it is too
late!"

Johnny's hand slipped down to grasp Maggie's in
a discreet squeeze. She was distracted enough to
look at her husband and caught the amusement in
his eyes. She felt little amusement herself. Had
Winslow actually been spying on them all? Were his
the footprints outside of Sam Thayer's wagon? If
so, why? Now he was shaking the Mormon bear at
them again. Would this preoccupation chase them
clear across the continent? The preacher's voice
drew her back again.

"Do not succumb! Put off the flesh that ye may be
purified! Co-mingling was meant for procreation
alone, procreation among God-fearing, monoga-
mous husband and wife!" His eyes again ran over
the group before him, stopping on women's faces,
as if to point out further offenders.

"As for drunkards, the Bible tells us they become
poor, become weighed down by their follies. They
see not the shining brass and gold of the Promised

Land, but are laid to waste by the lead of mere bullets." His eyes left the crowd for a moment, resting on the grave dramatically.

"Brother Richman has been laid to rest by the spirit, indeed. But not by the Spirit of God; rather, by the spirits of rum! He was begged by his good mother, pleaded with by his children, prayed over by myself. Did he reject that demon? No! He cradled it yet closer to his body, even as he lies cradling it beneath our feet today. And in choosing drunkenness, he chose Satan! He chose the path of least resistance. He chose the path which could have led all of us here today into death on this vast prairie, at the hands of the very heathen I come to save. Brother Richman was nearly our undoing!" The Reverend Winslow paused yet again before making complete his transformation into an avenging prophet.

"But in his downfall is our survival. In his downfall is a message from God Himself! Make thy shoes as iron and brass to keep yourselves from all temptations of the flesh. Use this time of tribulation as we cross the wilderness—much as the ancient Israelites did—use this time as a time of penance. Cleanse yourselves now! Cleanse yourselves by prayer and meditation, by putting away your riotous living, that when we reach the Promised Land, we may arrived purified in body and spirit!" He lowered his gaze to the body again.

"As for Brother Richman, perhaps his Faith was greater than his weak spirit. Perhaps even now he may be with Almighty God in heaven." Winslow inspected the mesmerized faces following his every word. His look suggested that his "perhaps" was a mighty long shot. "Let us pray that this may be so."

The Reverend Winslow bowed his head and there was a long moment of silence. Then the preacher strode away from the grave, leaving lesser men to cover the body with dirt.

There was a communal sigh before Grandma began singing "Washed in the Waters." Her voice rose high, with hardly a quaver, and slowly the others began taking it up, although one or two of the men muttered as to how the words should have been *washed* in something a little stronger.

The grave was right in the middle of the trail, and after it was filled, they ran a few wagons over Hal Richman, so the Indians wouldn't find him and dig him up for his clothing.

twelve

Nearly a week later, making a doggedly steady ten or twelve miles a day, the Chandler Party came into the Platte Basin, its members finally laying eyes on the river they would follow for the next six hundred miles. The whole train was called to an unusual midafternoon halt while the emigrants gawked like pleasure travelers.

Johnny came back to stand by Maggie and the children.

"That's it, then. We've made the first big piece—over three hundred miles."

Maggie took in the broad, shallow river, broken with sandbanks, then moved her eyes over the treeless plains of green surrounding them as far as the eye could see. "It has a certain beauty, Johnny, the grasses unbroken, unsoiled by any plow. It looks like it must have at the beginning of the world." The dust from the wagons had settled down, and she took a deep breath. "And the air. It's filled with the scent of blossoms. Millions of blossoms, Johnny."

"Yes, 'the bright consummate flower.' " He stooped to pick a sprig of blue and tucked it into her hair. His lips brushed her cheek.

"We will survive it, the next three hundred miles and beyond?"

"We'll make it, love."

Maggie gazed over the vast plains again. So much nothingness, yet so much fullness. "Will there be

141

more left behind to pay our dues? More splintered wagons, more graves?"

"Only God can answer that. But He did bring us this far, didn't He?"

They watched Jamie and the other children wandering over the knee-tall grass, gathering wildflowers. Jamie raced back at last to present a vibrant bouquet to his mother.

"They're lovely, son. Bless you for the thought."

He turned shy on her, rubbing one boot toe into the grass. "Ought to bring them for you more often, like Pa. You're even prettier with flowers about you."

Johnny was grinning as Maggie tipped up Jamie's face to give him a kiss. "And you're as handsome as your father when you bring them for me. There couldn't be two handsomer or nicer men in the entire world!"

Chandler's start-up signal floated down the line of wagons to be registered by her beaming men.

Maggie carefully tucked Jamie's bouquet into her waistband. She picked up Charlotte and pulled a fistful of yellow dandelion flowers from the child's mouth. "You're a little young yet for bouquets, my girl."

They began again.

Several days upon the Platte, and no buffalo had yet been sighted. Meat supplies were growing low. Firewood stashed in great piles atop belongings in the wagons had dwindled to nothing. The buffalo were not to be seen, but remnants of their passing became more evident. Children were sent out to gather the chips—more delicately called *bois de vache*—and fires began to smell strongly, more richly than the peat to which the chips were compared.

Maggie was sweating over her noonday fire when Gwen walked up.

"Feeling like an Israelite yet, Maggie?"

Maggie smiled. For several days following Winslow's vehement funeral address, the emigrants had walked around in a near state of shock. Now the jokes were beginning to float through the wagons.

"Not quite. But I'm beginning to think like one." She glanced pointedly at the pristinely blue sky. It had begun to get dry on the trail, very dry. "Does it look like any manna is about to appear from the heavens?"

Gwen followed her glance. "No. More's the pity." She pulled her skirts up a few inches and tried to separate the heavy cloth from her dripping body. "Is the prophet of doom anywhere in sight? I'd dearly love to cool my legs without being accused of wantonness."

Maggie let out a peal of laughter. "You're progressing, Gwen. A few weeks back, you would've denied that a lady's appendages actually existed."

Gwen squatted down next to Maggie. "I did mention my ankles in mixed company, you might recall."

"Yes, with more than a few blushes." Maggie grinned as she noted Gwen redden again. "Where is your stalwart suitor? Hasn't he been sharing the noon meal with you and Irish lately?"

"He has, at that. And he's been growing bolder, too. He even suggested that we might begin the daily ritual properly by joining him for breakfast at his fire."

"The man is smitten, indeed. Will you?"

"Will I what? Oh, the breakfast business. I'm not convinced I've progressed that far. A maiden lady requires *some* privacy. Besides, morning is not my best time. The little mirror I brought shows all sorts of insufficiencies in my visage in those early hours—lines and wrinkles I tend to forget with the sweat and dust of the day. But I daresay they're still there."

Gwen fanned at her face. "Dear me, but I wish for some of my old skin creams. What I wouldn't do for the juice of a single cucumber! Even with a bonnet continually in place, my complexion looks closer to an Indian squaw's!"

"Never mind." Maggie grinned. "Sam doesn't seem to care. At least you don't sprout freckles like I do!"

Johnny walked up then, covered with a fine white dust, heading for the water bag. "What's this about freckles, ladies? It appears to me that a freckle would not stand a chance of being seen under all of this dust." He doused his head thoroughly, then shook it in a close approximation of a wet Bacon. "I haven't decided what's worse yet, mud or dust. Notice how they both tend to cling, though? Just like a phrase you can't get out of your mind, or an acquaintance you'd rather not meet."

Maggie picked up on his thought. "Who's been

cornering you, Johnny?"

He sank down next to her and made a slight grimace at the frying pan. "Pancakes again? And we've run out of molasses."

"Honey, too. Not to mention bacon."

Gwen's expression turned guilty, and she quickly rose. "We've some honey left, Maggie. And a slab of bacon, too. Irish and I are overdue on contributions."

"We'd be much obliged, Gwen." Maggie turned her attention back to her husband. "What's going on, Johnny? You know I haven't time to gossip. It must come from you."

"Jed Smith, Al Jarboe, and Martin Simpson."

She waited. Then, prodding him on, "Yes?"

"They're giving Chandler a hard time. Questioning his captaincy. Pushing him to travel on the other side of the Platte."

"Why, Johnny? It just means another dangerous fording. The Platte looks shallow, but I've been watching some vicious currents."

"Maybe quicksand, too. But the grass always looks greener on the other side. I don't think they'll do it, Meg, but the dissension so early in the trip puts strains on the whole train."

"What does Chandler say?"

"The novelty of his captaincy has begun to wear off. 'Uneasy lies the head that wears the crown,' as Shakespeare put it. He just shrugs and says he can't make anybody stay against their will."

Maggie thought while she tended her dinner. "Has our progress been that slow? The oxen can only be pressed so far. As it is, they get unruly toward the end of the day. They just seem to know that they shouldn't be pushed farther."

"Mules and horses would have been faster, without our heavy possessions. We'd be at Fort Laramie already, another three hundred miles along."

Maggie studied her husband. He was older from the month on the trail. The responsibilities were making him more of a realist, less of a dreamer. She'd never thought of him as a leader of men before. This was changing. The strong tan on his face and the strengthened muscles were becoming, too. Would he arrive in the Territory a different man? Maybe they would all be different.

"We can't worry about Simpson and Jarboe, Johnny. You know they'll do what they decide to do, no matter what we say."

"That's the pity of it." He lay on his back and stared into the sky. "It will be clear again tonight. It's time to start Jamie on astronomy lessons. Constellations, and the North Star."

Maggie watched him lying there. "May I join the class, teacher, or am I too old?"

"You're never too old to learn, Meg, love. Never even too old to change one's ways, if your mind is strong enough. Most folks just don't want to, more's the shame." He watched her at her tasks, then beckoned her over. "Then again, some things just get better with repetition. Like the noon greeting I almost forgot."

He rose halfway to meet her lips and Maggie sank down to settle his head on her lap, accepting the rare moment of love.

thirteen

The astronomy lessons did not begin that night. Instead, the travelers had a social call from the Pawnees who had been following them. The band of horsemen began raising dust on the horizon just before sunset, and appeared at the camp entirely too soon thereafter. Their rifles were unraised, so the skittish camp had to assume that the visit was to be a peaceful one.

The women and children were ordered to the rear as usual—in this case, one side of the circled corral of wagons—while the men hovered together protectively at the far side to meet the intruders.

Trust Jamie to sneak away toward the action, Maggie noted with a frown of concern.

He returned a few minutes later, all excitement. "Ma! Ma! You'll never guess!"

Maggie had that old strange tingle in her spine again, but tried to appear as calm as possible. "Jamie, you were told to stay with me!"

"Sorry, Ma, but you know what they want?" He could hardly contain his news.

"More food?"

"Their leader, the one all dressed up, his name is Red Eagle. He speaks English! He says he comes to see the strong woman whose hair is like the setting sun, and whose eyes flash like the lightning!"

Maggie felt her stomach sink with a thud, while Hazel and Gwen gave her terrified looks.

"May the Lord have mercy. You're the only one with red hair, Maggie." Hazel stared at her with awe, fingering her own black bun with unbridled relief.

"Oh, no!" wailed Gwen. "They're walking this way!"

Maggie tried to pull her eyes away from the stew pot, but the jackrabbit Sam had bagged for their dinner took on a sudden fascination. She stirred the cauldron with her wooden spoon several times, unnecessarily.

"They really are, Maggie!" Hazel backed away nervously, grabbing her children.

Maggie picked up the wandering Charlotte and handed her to Gwen. "Hold the baby for me, please. And Jamie, you stay out of harm's way, hear?"

His eyes were wide. "Yes, ma'am."

Maggie finally found the courage to raise her head. She was alone. Abandoned. The other women had scampered away like frightened sparrows. She couldn't find it in her heart to blame them. She herself would prefer running. But she did not. She stood straight and proud, waiting for her husband and Chandler to finish escorting Red Eagle to the Stuart campsite.

Their walk across the center of the circle seemed to take forever. Johnny was walking tall, and she could see he was thinking hard. A frown of concentration filled his face. And then they were standing before her.

"Meg," Johnny spoke first. "Meg, this is Red Eagle, chief of his band of Pawnee."

Maggie stood stock still before the man, taking him in. Was she supposed to shake hands with him? It did seem to be a formal introduction. She felt the nerves in her fingers twitching with the effort to make the decision. To move or not to move. Finally, she willed her right hand still, and nodded her head.

The man was handsome, in a primitive way. As tall as Johnny, he was got up in what certainly appeared to be his fanciest outfit—soft, decorated buckskin, and an imposing headdress of feathers that reached far down his back. His high, smooth cheekbones outlined a face deeply bronzed, punctuated by a strongly hooked nose, and eyes that were black, but appeared as sharp and merciless as his namesake's.

"Red Eagle," Johnny continued, "was told of you by one of his braves. It must have been the one that kicked Bacon—"

"I will speak now," interrupted the Indian.

Johnny took a halfstep away, and nodded acquiescence.

The Indian's eyes were fixed on Maggie's hair, glowing in the last rays of the dying sun. His hand lifted now to touch it.

"My special medicine is red. I am Red Eagle." He gestured to the signs painted on his covered chest, pointing things out. "The sun. Coming up. Going down. The birds who hunt. You will be good medicine for me. You will be my wife."

"But—" Maggie sputtered.

He silenced her. "It will be. It is written in the heavens." He motioned toward the still-falling sun.

It did seem to be taking its time tonight, almost hesitating in place before making its final journey below the horizon. "Look. The sun waits to smile longer upon you, to let me look upon you again."

He turned to Johnny. "I trade you for this woman. Make good trade, in good faith. Ten horses."

Johnny blanched.

"Twelve horses."

Gathering his courage, Johnny answered. "I would rather not trade her, sir. I am quite accustomed to her, you understand. She is a good cook, a good mother to our children."

Red Eagle considered this. "Good woman maybe worth more. Fourteen horses. Final offer. I have horses here. Take her with me now."

Maggie stared at Johnny, longing to be within the protection of his arms. His tanned face had gone white. He was beginning to believe how deadly serious this Indian really was. At the same time, she knew he was struggling mightily to find the proper words to keep the discussion amicable, not to insult the chief. She could also see Chandler in the background. He was fondling his rifle, bristling.

"We have a baby, a girl-child," Johnny tried. "The baby needs her mother's milk."

"Bring baby here!"

The Indian spoke the words with such authority that Maggie quivered. *Please God, don't let the children get involved in this!*

Johnny, deeply troubled, motioned Gwen out of the background shadows. She advanced very tentatively, clutching Charlotte as if she were her own daughter. Red Eagle inspected the child carefully, touching her hair, poking in her ears, even thrusting a finger into her mouth. Maggie tried to control herself, but one more poke would have had her screaming.

The Indian finally waved Gwen and Charlotte away. "Will take girl-baby, but no more horses."

Johnny shuffled his feet uncomfortably and tried again. "Then there's our son. He would be sorely tried by his mother's absence."

"Bring boy!"

Jamie edged from behind the wagon of his own accord and walked up manfully. Red Eagle went through the same process, but when he thrust a finger into the boy's mouth to check his teeth, Jamie bit him, hard. The Indian held his bitten finger gravely, and Maggie could have sworn she saw the ghost of a smile in the man's eyes.

"Take boy, too. Give one pony for him." He turned from Johnny as if the subject were closed.

Johnny ran a hand through his curly hair. He was sweating with the effort of the challenge before him. "Red Eagle." The authority in his voice caught the Indian's attention. He swerved back to face Johnny again.

"We are both men, and can talk like men. Your offer for my family is a great honor. Fourteen horses is a great many horses for a mere woman, even an extraordinary woman, as my woman is. One pony is fair for the boy. He is a good boy. As the baby is yet a baby, her worth is unknown. Your offer to accept her is also fair." Johnny paused to further summon his thoughts.

"Unfortunately, this woman and these children are great medicine for me, too. Without them, I would lose my own strength. I would sicken and die. To die from the loss of one's medicine is not the way for a man to die. A man should die in battle. He should die honorably, by fighting his foes." He waited to observe the effect of his words.

A gleam of understanding began to show in the Indian's eyes. Johnny took heart and continued. "We are both men, so can understand this thing. I cannot live without these people, and I do not wish to die less than a man. I cannot accept the offer you make in good faith. Many horses may make a man rich in belongings, but many horses cannot cure the sickness here." Johnny held a clenched fist evocatively over his heart. "It is better to remain poor and keep one's honor with the Great Spirit."

"You know the Great Spirit?"

"I do. I have words and pictures from the Great Spirit Himself."

The Indian started. "How can that be?"

Johnny held the Pawnee chief's eyes. "Not all white men are concerned only with destroying that which the Great Spirit has given us. There are some who study the good things around us. They put them into words and pictures."

Johnny was slowly moving toward the book wagon. Now he reached it, unfastened the side hooks, and carefully opened his display of books. His hand went unerringly to a large volume. He pulled it out and brought it close to the light from the fire. "Come. See."

Maggie gasped. Johnny had chosen his most trea-
sured book, a folio volume of Audubon's birds.
He'd searched long and bargained hard to get it. Her
husband stooped near the fire to gain more light
upon the pages, and motioned for the Indian to
follow. In a moment they were squatting almost
companionably next to each other, the Indian's eyes
widening as he registered the lovingly drawn
pictures.

"This book," Johnny motioned, "this book contains many wonders, the likeness of many birds of
the air. It even contains the likeness of your own
namesake." Miraculously, Johnny turned to a picture of an eagle. The Indian grunted.

Johnny locked into the chief's eyes. "Its worth is
more than fifteen horses. Its worth is more than
many, many buffalo robes."

Red Eagle nodded in understanding.

Johnny turned several more pages. Finally, ritual-
istically, he closed the book and put it into the
chief's hands. "This is my gift to you. You will be a
great chief with this book. You will be able to look
upon the eagle and his brothers whenever you wish . . .
and I will keep my family and my medicine. I will
keep my soul."

Apparently accepting the offer, Red Eagle nodded
and rose. The sun had finally set, leaving lingering
streaks of vermillion slashed across the western sky.
He glanced off at his braves hovering at the edge of
the falling darkness. Following his unspoken instructions, they began to move out of the circle of

the wagons, toward their waiting horses.

The chief turned once more. "What is your name, you who understand the Great Spirit?"

"John Stuart."

"Stew-ert. So." And Red Eagle, too, was gone.

The camp retained a deathly silence until the hoofbeats of the Indians' horses echoed far into the distance.

At last, Chandler eased up on the death grip he'd held on his rifle. He came forward to clap Johnny on the back. "I never figured words could take the place of bullets. Nor books, neither. But them books of yours come through just fine. Well done, Stuart. It was a mite tetchy there for a while."

"Yes, sir, it was."

Trembling, Johnny went to Maggie and took her into his arms. They held each other until they felt strong enough to speak. Johnny pulled out of the embrace first, trying to make light of the incident. "I just declared you were a good cook. I hope the dinner wasn't ruined by this little affair."

"Little affair, my foot! But I should not even be looking upon you. I'm a mere woman, after all, while *you* converse regularly with the Great Spirit!"

He pulled her back into his arms. "But you are my medicine! And never forget that I gave up fourteen good horses for you." He touched her hair wonderingly. "Like the sunset and the sunrise you are to me, indeed. The Indians can teach me a few things about loving you, Meg. . . . I was so afraid of losing you!"

Jamie shot out of the shadows to hug at Maggie's

skirts, unwilling to let go. Charlotte was thrust into her arms, crying for her dinner. The whole world—at least the small world of the camp—was upon the Stuarts, chattering with excitement and congratulations.

All but the Reverend Winslow, who stood aside with his family, an "I told you so" expression upon his face, and in his heart the knowledge that his prophecies were beginning to take place.

fourteen

Spurred by the latest Pawnee visit, the train fairly flew across the plains over the next days. The stock could always quench its thirst in the Platte, but the emigrants were delighted to come upon Cottonwood Springs, the last pure water for several hundred miles. They camped at twilight, and Chandler sent word from wagon to wagon that the next day would be one of rest.

Maggie lay under their tent that night, trying to fight off swarms of mosquitoes and gnats that had descended out of nowhere. She finally pulled herself up, sweaty and uncomfortable in her nightgown. Johnny was on guard duty and she missed him.

Hardly thinking, she gathered her shawl around her and began to unbutton the tent flaps. She was feeling so restless. She'd just wander down to the spring to bathe in privacy. It might cool her off—her body as well as her mind.

Swatting at the constant drone in her ear, Maggie tiptoed between the wagons, hugging the gown and shawl to her. Best to check in with the nearest night watch first, although how she could be mistaken for an Indian eluded her.

She searched, eyes adjusting to the star-filled night. Bother! The Reverend Winslow had duty on the side nearest the spring. That gaunt, hawklike form couldn't be mistaken. Why couldn't it have

156

been Johnny? Winslow had spotted her now, though, and she couldn't very well retreat. The two figures moved within a respectable ten yards of each other.

"Good evening, Reverend."

He nodded curtly.

"I won't disturb you. I'm just going to the spring to refresh myself. The night is so warm."

He shifted his rifle to slap at a swarm of insects hovering over him. Even his cloak of sanctity wasn't sufficient to keep him in a halo of air free from the hungry creatures. "It's against regulations. I must ask you to return to your wagon."

"Oh, for goodness sake. You know where I'll be. There's but one cottonwood on the whole plain before us, and you can see most of it from here."

"Nevertheless—"

"I'm going. If you bump into Johnny, you may tell him."

She started walking off, but his low, grating voice caused her to hesitate. "Were I your master, I would husband you more carefully."

"You're not my master, nor is any other earthly man. Johnny is my husband, chosen by free will, and I'll not stand out here debating this or any other matter with you all night. I'm going to the spring." Picking up the skirt of her nightgown, Maggie rushed on.

Once at the spring, hidden by the lone tree, Maggie shook her head in defiance, shrugged off her shawl, and knelt down to scoop the deliciously cold water over her face and arms. In the haste of her sudden decision, she'd not thought to bring soap, or even a drying cloth. Small matter. She'd linger here a while to dry in the small gully whose gravel bed moved on, right into the Platte.

Refreshed, she stood, her water-dappled face and arms outlined against the sky. Maggie took in the night's sudden goodness—the sliver of a moon beginning to wane, the bright constellations she could now name after the last few nights of Johnny's lessons. And streaking through the very center of this sky was something bright, shiny, effervescent.

Could it be a falling star? She'd seen only one before. It had been midsummer's night in Ohio, when she was fourteen. She'd been sitting on the porch with Johnny. He'd been telling her about the magic of that special night, recounting stories from Shakespeare about Puck and Titania and Bottom. He'd whispered in her ear, too. Shy words that couldn't possibly have been spoken in the bold light of day. The words had been thrilling to a girl-child on the brink of womanhood, sitting with her beloved. It was the one night of the year that anything could happen, he promised—to lovers.

That was the first time she'd laid her head on Johnny's shoulder, though she'd dreamed of it through the long winter before his coming. It was the first time he'd ventured to throw his arm around her, tentatively, innocently. There was a yellow moon beginning to disappear through the trees. That's when they'd seen the falling star. But Johnny had called it a *rising* star. Oh stars, these blessed candles of the night. *Their* star.

Maggie made a sudden pirouette in the prairie night, as star-struck and lovesick again as she had been at fourteen. Perhaps Johnny was watching this same star with her now, from the other side of the camp.

Her arms, raised to the heavens, fell suddenly to her sides. An unexpected quiver ran through her spine, bringing her eyes back to the earth. The quiver wasn't caused by thoughts of Johnny or even of that long-ago night. Maggie suddenly felt, suddenly knew that something or someone else was watching in this night, and it was not watching the stars.

She reached for her shawl and pulled it over her shoulders, hiding her body which had not felt chilled until this moment. Could it be Winslow? She peered through the branches of the cottonwood, toward camp. The women had continued to carry tales of him. He seemed always to be where least expected, least wanted, always when their men were busy elsewhere. And at such moments, his expression had suggested anything but pure thoughts.

Maggie peered around intently. The grasses, now almost thigh-high, could hide practically anything. The jackrabbits would be sleeping, and the snakes, too. Perhaps a fox? There was a sudden movement, but it came from behind her.

She spun around to stare into the face of an Indian. The face was painted with long stripes across the cheekbones, and it took precious seconds to distinguish it as that of Red Eagle.

Maggie's eyes widened with sudden recognition,

sudden understanding. Her mouth opened to cry for help, but it was too late. A dark hand was clapped across her lips, and before she could bite that hand, it was replaced by a ragged strip of rawhide, tied firmly behind her head.

Maggie was bodily hauled over a shoulder, kicking and scratching. When her silent protests began to annoy her captor, she was tossed to the earth, to be dragged through the tall grasses by her long red hair, her passing marked only by a flattened strip of turf, a strip the soft breezes gradually righted.

Johnny was relieved at midnight. He strode quickly back to his tent, anticipating his wife and his rest, nodding to Winslow heading toward his own tent and wife.

Unexpectedly, Winslow delayed him. "You'd best put some fear of the Lord into that wife of yours, Stuart."

Johnny stared without understanding. "What are you talking about?"

"It be indecent for a woman to be wandering around the camp and beyond at night, dressed in naught but her nightclothes."

"Meg?" He blinked, then raced to his tent to peek in. She wasn't there. He sped to the book wagon, checking the children and the pup, all blissfully asleep. As a final shot, he ran to the white-top, clambered in, and managed to crack both knees on the Ramage press. His exhaustion was suddenly gone, replaced by cold fear.

Johnny returned to Winslow, grabbing at the man

as he was pulling off his boots. "Where is she, Winslow? Where's my wife? Where did you see her last? When?"

Winslow shrugged out of Johnny's grip. "But an hour past. Going to the spring to *refresh* herself."

"You let her pass? And you said naught to me? Are you out of your mind, man?"

Johnny's freed hands had balled up, and he was on the verge of doing severe damage to Winslow's aristocratic nose.

The preacher had the sense to look frightened before he pulled his dignity together. "I am not the keeper of my brother's wife. I gave her fair warning. If she chose to ignore it, as she has ignored my countless other words of Christian advice on her behalf, it is none of my business."

"But she didn't come back! Surely you would have looked for her return!"

"I was pacing a different area by then. I thought she had returned."

Johnny wasted no more words. Instead, he flew to the spring, stopping short before reaching the damp area around it. He must calm down, look for signs.

He found them. There were scuffled footprints— partially his wife's bare feet, partially a moccasined foot. There was also a feather. He picked it up, trying to distinguish its form in the night. It was long and full and could not belong to any ordinary bird of the plains. He would check it by lamplight, but in his heart Johnny knew it was the feather of an eagle.

fifteen

The rising sun found Maggie astride an Indian pony, her hands tied behind her back, her body fettered by an intricate system of ropes Red Eagle had used to chain her to the animal. She ached over every inch of her frame from the long dragging she'd endured during her abduction from the spring. It had seemed to last forever, but was perhaps only the course of a half mile— as far as the bluff which stood, outlined darkly against the night sky to the south of the wagons.

Hidden behind the bluff had been two waiting horses, and her captor had lost no time in placing her securely on her mount, then urging on both animals. At first, he'd led the two horses at a walk. Sounds travel quickly over the empty night prairies. Soon he was prodding them into a steady trot. Too many miles had been covered in the distance between the midnight and the dawn.

Maggie sat astride her horse with as much iron in her spine as she could muster, but her whirring mind kept telling her that it was to little purpose. Red Eagle meant to have his way, and Johnny was too far to save her.

Yet, aside from the flailing of her limbs through the grasses, the Pawnee had been surprisingly gentle. He could have taken advantage of her by the bluff, or anywhere since. Could have cast her aside, to wander back to the camp to face the degradation newly befallen her.

Why hadn't he taken advantage? Did he really mean to marry her? She gazed at his back wonderingly as he finally slowed both horses.

Red Eagle pulled her horse up next to his and pointed from the rise on which they stood. "My village."

Below them was a circle of huts, low and rounded, made of mud and wattles. Even though she saw her future staring bleakly back at her, Maggie couldn't help being taken by the sight. It was foreign to everything she knew, yet still fascinating. Unable to speak, she concentrated on counting the huts. The numbers kept her mind from straying to what must come next, kept her from praying the same prayer for deliverance that had focused her mind through the night's dark ride. There were twenty distinct "houses," one of which was somewhat larger than the others.

He saw her gaze rest on it. "My lodge." He said it with pride. "My wives will be waking now, preparing my food."

Maggie swallowed, hard. She tried to focus on the few straggly dogs she saw stretching in the dry dust around fires that would soon be rekindled.

How many other wives had he? How would they respond to her? Would they have children, babies, like her own? And who would feed Charlotte in her absence? She'd been struggling with that question all night, mixing it in with her prayers. And each time she thought of her daughter, she would feel her chest tightening.

Maggie glanced away from the village, down to her

soiled and torn nightdress. She was still decently covered, but patches of moisture from perspiration stained her nightgown. She felt very uncomfortable.

Red Eagle followed her eyes. "Weather change soon. Heat will end. You will feel better."

Tears came to Maggie's eyes, but she could not brush them away. He took small pity on her and released the gag from her mouth.

"What do you want with me?" Maggie whispered.

"As before. Wife. Book of Great Spirit is good, but now I have both. Is better. My medicine will be very strong. When I returned from hunt—hunt for you—my village was displeased. They think I go for making war. Before I leave with all the many horses, they sing war song over me."

He looked over the village, into the slowly lightening skies to the east, and slowly chanted:

> *Is this real,*
> *this life I live?*
> *Is this real,*
> *this life I live?*

He turned to her again. "War makes life real. When doubt comes, it is time to go on the path of war once again. But my village was displeased with my return. No new scalps of honor. Even the Book did not make their minds to change."

He paused in thought. "But me, I do not need to prove myself a man in war yet again. I have done so many times. I want only a new wife. One that will give me children with hair like the sun, eyes like fire of the summer storm. They will be strong and brave, our sons."

Maggie could hardly believe her ears. In his own way, the Indian was telling her he loved her. She couldn't pull her eyes from his strong face, even though she knew it was inappropriate by his standards and an insult to those left behind at the camp. Feeling like a traitor, she cast her eyes away, but not before they'd locked with the Indian's.

He grunted at the look, then sang out something softly in his own language. The words were sharp, yet musical:

> I think,
>> oh, I think
> I have found
>> my lover at last.
> I think it is so.

He slid off his horse, undid the bonds of her hands and body, then mounted again. "You will enter my village as my wife-to-be. Not as a common slave. Come."

He kicked his horse and led her down the slope.

Johnny had returned to the wagons like a madman. He woke his friends selectively, but soon the entire camp was up, creating a scene more frenzied than the night of Hal Richman's death.

He'd woken the Krellers first, begging Hazel's mercies to look after Jamie and nurse Charlotte in his absence. Bleary-eyed and disbelieving, Hazel had sworn to care for his children like her own.

That settled, Johnny had gone to saddle Dickens and Miss Sally.

Max had stopped him. "Those dray animals have the stamina but not the speed you'll be needing, Johnny. Take my stallion, and one of my mares for Maggie. I'll follow along with another horse."

"No! I must do this thing alone!"

"You be out of your mind, Stuart," threw in Josh Chandler as he pulled on the boots he'd carried to Johnny's wagon. "It's a posse we'll be needin'."

Sam nodded gravely in the background, while Irish stood moving his weight from one unshod foot to the other nervously.

"We don't even know which direction they've gone." Irish's voice was plaintive in its fear.

"It must be south. Crossing the river would have alerted Winslow and me. They came afoot, but could only leave horses hidden near that bluff." Johnny pointed at the shape in the night. "I must start by the bluff and track them."

"And what books are you thinkin' will save you this time, Stuart?" Chandler's eyes by lamplight had fury in them. "Nothin'll get you out of this one but bullets."

"No guns. No bullets. My wife could be hurt." Johnny finished saddling the stallion and mounted. "You rest tomorrow, which is to the good. If we have not returned by the next morning, you're to go on without us. We'll catch up." And he was gone.

"Ready your horses," Chandler ordered the men around him. "Let him get the half mile to the bluff, and we'll follow behind. He'll be blessing us for our support if he don't get himself killed first."

The group of men nodded in agreement and sprang into action.

The village came alive as Maggie entered it. A low murmur in a foreign tongue surrounded her. Naked children scampered from their huts to be followed by their mothers, and finally by a frightening array of braves. The men stood, arms folded and sullen, sternly contemplating Red Eagle's folly, while the women buzzed around the captive who would bring excitement to their village. All but two.

Maggie noticed the two Pawnee women standing by the entrance to Red Eagle's lodge. They were arrayed in plain, short, buckskin dresses, simple moccasins on their feet. His other wives. They were both darkly attractive—the taller, older one with a face that would have been lovely had it not been ravaged by the smallpox; the younger one, perhaps no more than fifteen. Their faces were not sullen, as they could have been. They were frightened.

Frightened of what? Maggie wondered to herself. She glanced upon them again and saw the looks they gave their husband, next to her. Suddenly Maggie understood. They were frightened of losing him. They both loved him. This discovery made Maggie feel even worse. Not only was she dragged here against her will, but she would now become—helplessly—a thorn in Red Eagle's family and tribal relations. Were she unable to escape, she would have to fight off not only his advances, but also what would surely grow into the unbridled enmity of his senior wives.

The tableau remained unchanged for a few seconds. Before they could dismount, however, one of the braves stepped forward. Maggie gasped as she recognized Bacon's attacker. His eyes pierced hers with unbridled lechery which quickly changed to hatred as he confronted his chief. He addressed Red Eagle with little deference, showing his displeasure in every body movement. Red Eagle listened, finally turning to Maggie. "This man is Snake Who Bites. He is trouble. Stay away."

With no further ado, and without even pausing to answer Snake's grievances, the chief dismounted. He helped Maggie down, and led her, stumbling, to his lodge.

He spoke briefly to his waiting women before turning to explain. "These are my wives." He thought a moment, trying to translate their names. "This," he nodded to the taller of the two, "is Corn Girl, and this," looking at the shorter, younger one, "Evening Star." They will clean and prepare you for the marriage feast. It will be tonight." He turned away. "I go now to hunt for the feast. Should we travel longer than I hope, the ceremony will wait for my return."

Maggie was led by the two women into the dark, smoky interior of the hut. She gazed around her in dismay. On a raised ledge to one side were piles of buffalo robes, still reeking of the animals who had once worn them. They must be the beds. Aside from the ledge, there were occasional baskets strung up around the wall, dried meats and vegetables, and not much else.

She stared into the small central fire, not knowing what would be expected of her next. Sounds of gathering horses filtered into the lodge from outside. They galloped off, out of the village. She had an urge to run after them, to beg Red Eagle not to leave her alone here.

Her aching body brought her back to reality. What was to be done? What would become of her, of her children, of her husband? Close to despair, Maggie sank onto her knees on the hard-packed dirt floor, buried her head in her hands, and prayed.

sixteen

Morning light found Johnny riding hard, always for the south. He was not an outdoorsman, but even he could follow the tracks left by Red Eagle through the plains grasses. The Indian had been either very sure of himself, or very much in a hurry to get his prize home. Perhaps both. Johnny castigated himself continuously for not keeping a closer eye on his wife, for believing, in pride, that his "superior intelligence" had outsmarted the red man during their last encounter.

As he grew wearier and more worried, his thoughts actually turned upon blaming Maggie. He'd never blamed her for anything, never even quarreled with her before. But now he had a genuine bone to pick with the woman.

Her nocturnal swim reminded him of a scene he'd read once. Wasn't it a beautiful woman named Bathsheba who had taken a bath on a rooftop in Jerusalem, stirring the passions of King David? And hadn't that innocent exhibition led to adultery, then murder? If even King David, "the man after God's own heart," could be guilty of such crimes, then what might an uncivilized Indian do when confronted with a woman like Maggie?

What right had she to discount her beauty so completely? Had she no idea of what her charms could do to other men? Had she really any idea of what she did to himself?

Thou has ravished my heart, my sister, my spouse; thou hast ravished my heart with one of thine eyes, with one chain of thy neck. . . . how much better is thy love than wine! and the smell of thine ointments than all spices!

When the stallion raised his head questioningly, Johnny realized he'd been thinking aloud, quoting the Bible* into a land of sudden darkness, and of the shadow of death. Such this wilderness would become to him without his beloved. Had he ever told Meg her worth to him? Surely not often enough.

Self-doubt set in as Johnny realized that *he* could be responsible for the hiding of Maggie's light under a bushel. Could it be jealousy of other men? He'd never considered himself a jealous man. He'd just taken it all for granted. Meg's beauty, her unconditional love for him—without strings of any sort—her total trust in him.

"Trust!" He growled the word aloud, then yelled it into the brightening sky. "Trust!"

She had entrusted her life into his hands, and what had he done? Dragged her away from a perfectly respectable, perfectly safe life in the East to fulfill his own selfish need for wandering.

Johnny castigated himself thus for another mile or so, resolving that when he got his woman back, a few things would change. The first being that she take a close look at herself and proceed accordingly. No more taking things for granted.

---

*Song of Solomon 4:9-10 (KJV).

He'd get her back, all right. He had no doubts on that account. *How* he'd get her back was another matter entirely. His mind and pulse were rushing too quickly to consider the hows with any intelligence. Not Shakespeare nor any of his books could help him now. All his quotes spread from here to Oregon would not make an ounce of difference. Unless it was some bit of divine wisdom that could help him in his hour of need. For only God knew where Maggie was and what was befalling her at this moment.

Steadier, Johnny studied the early morning sky. His mind must be clear and clean. It must be elemental, like that of his foe. For once, Johnny Stuart must become a man of complete action. He'd find her and he'd take her. That was that.

Gentle hands touched Maggie's shoulders, her face, her hair. She looked up into the eyes of the two women. They were comforting now, sympathetic. The tall one, Corn Girl, gestured toward an open clay bowl nearby that Maggie's first glance had missed. Water. She moved toward it and drank, then tried to splash it over her body. They stopped her. She stared at them, not comprehending. Slowly they pulled the destroyed gown over her head. Soothing noises came from their throats as they saw the bruises beginning to darken her body. With care and compassion Red Eagle's two wives began to bathe her.

Corn Girl stared at her understandingly. She made motions of rocking a baby. Maggie nodded as tears came to her eyes again. She gestured toward what she felt was the direction of the camp, the direction of her baby daughter.

Corn Girl traced a tear moving down Maggie's face and pointed to a cradleboard sitting empty against the side of the hut. She made digging and burying motions. She had had a baby once. It had died. Maggie reached out her hand and felt Corn Girl's scarred cheeks. Had the smallpox taken her baby? At her touch, the woman nodded yes. Understanding was reached in the mutual grief of two women who had lost their children.

Soon she was clothed again, this time in a buckskin dress that obviously belonged to the taller woman. It must be her fancy dress, for it was fringed and beaded lovingly. Maggie forgot her predicament for a long moment to admire its decorations, to smile her approval into the eyes of its owner. Corn Girl smiled back, then blushed. Evening Star brought Maggie a bowl of corn mush, and she ate.

Finally Maggie was prepared and led outside the lodge. The village was now deserted save for two braves obviously on sentry duty and several ancient women who sat hunched over primitive stone mortar and pestles, laboriously grinding corn into flour.

One of the braves turned. Maggie's heart dropped. It was Snake. They stared into each other's eyes for a defiant moment before Evening Star pulled impatiently at Maggie.

Where were they leading her? They hurried, passing through the village quickly, then to the west, and

Maggie understood.

Fields of young corn and squash spread out before her. Moving slowly between the rows were women and young girls with hoeing sticks. A few of them carried water pots that they shared sparingly, lovingly, with each individual plant. Maggie heard whoops of excitement and looked beyond the fields to where the boys were, playing war games, practicing with their bows and arrows.

The village seemed to be well organized. These were far from primitive people. Each person had his own job. The boy-child must study to become a hunter and warrior, the girl-child to carry on the planting and housekeeping tasks of the community. Maggie's appreciation was short-lived, however, because Evening Star was approaching, handing her a heavy jug and gesturing that watering was to be her duty.

Maggie accepted her chore. She must gain the trust of the women. If she were a good worker, she would be more readily accepted into their society. She would make their labor less, and thus be appreciated. She must play the game. She must elicit their trust. But tonight she would escape. Before the feast. Before the wedding.

She chose a parched row of struggling young corn and set into her task.

Johnny halted to rest his horses. There were two sets of tracks before him, diverging. Should he take the one bearing farther south, or the one to the west? Could he tell which tracks were the more recent?

He'd dismounted and was bending over the plains before him, considering, when he heard the sound of approaching horses. He raised his head, fully expecting to see Josh Chandler and his posse coming to meet him. He'd known he couldn't keep Chandler at the camp for long. Johnny shaded his eyes and squinted into the rising sun.

"No! It's not possible!"

The words thrust from his mouth with fury. Shock and confusion assailed him. It was not Chandler, but the Pawnee themselves! Johnny reached up to his saddle for his rifle, only to remember that he'd chosen not to bring it. God help him. What now?

Visions of Maggie being an Indian captive for life beset him. The nightmare of their two children left completely orphaned chased behind the first thought. What choice had he? Had he any choice?

The horses bore down, their hooves vibrating the ground beneath his feet. Johnny stood tall to meet the enemy.

Maggie had been watering for several hours, and the midmorning heat was becoming oppressive. She glanced toward the other women. Some sang softly to themselves, others paused to give directives to their daughters, or reach a reassuring hand to steady the papooses on their backs. None seemed wearied. Then again, none of them had been up all night, being abducted across the plains.

Maggie bowed low with her jug to deal with the next cornstalk. It was a wretchedly incompetent way to keep the plants alive. Hadn't anyone explained the principles of irrigation to these people? That little stream flowing nearby, the one where the jugs were filled. It could quite easily be dammed. Channels could be dug to open into each row of the Pawnee fields. Lifegiving water would flow freely. The village women would be able to plant more, closer together. They would have a better and bigger crop. Why, if her father could spend one week with these people, their ways of farming could be changed forever, to the better.

A picture of Maggie's strong, ascetic father crept into her mind. He was frowning. James McDonald would not approve of his eldest daughter spending the rest of her natural life among the heathen— married to one! And without the benefit of widowhood. As against her will as a marriage to Red Eagle might be, her father could only interpret it as living in sin. A fate worse than death.

Maggie paused, jug in hand, between sprouts. Was it really a fate worse than death? No. Nothing was worse than death, she thought, at least now, while she still had so much to live for. Death was too final, even with heaven on the other side. Try as she might, Maggie could not consider death as an alternative to her current plight. She must never despair, though like Paul, she be "pressed out of measure, above strength." She must trust in God for deliverance.

With Him, there was always hope. Hope for finding Johnny and her children again. She'd find them if she had to walk in their wake alone the next fifteen hundred miles. She'd walked the first piece, hadn't she? Nothing could keep her from the hope that they would eventually make it to Oregon, together. Death would never find her willingly.

At that, Maggie felt an inordinate heat overtake her body. She collapsed into a dead swoon, her water jug cracked and abandoned at her side.

Johnny stood his ground while the hunting party circled. Finally they stopped, and Red Eagle confronted him. "Stew-ert. Why you trespass on our grounds?"

"You know. You have something that belongs to me."

The Indian feigned innocence. "The Book of the Great Spirit was a gift."

"True. But my wife was not!"

"Trading over. No more horses." Red Eagle made a motion to swing his mount away.

"I don't want the horses! I want my wife! And I shall get her!"

The Indian stayed his horse and those of the others with a simple motion of his hand. "Talk easy. I kill you now, she is mine." He raised his rifle.

Johnny stood firm. "Is that the way of Pawnee warriors? To shoot a man who has no weapons? A man defenseless? I thought your honor was above that."

"Sometimes honor is too much trouble." But the bore of the rifle lowered an inch.

Johnny, grasping the only opportunity available to him, talked fast.

"Red Eagle, in my world we have a way to settle

such disputes between men and their property, men and their women. Perhaps you have something like it in yours." He paused and the Indian nodded that he was still listening. Johnny continued. "It is a way to settle things with complete honor. We call it a duel."

Red Eagle raised an eyebrow quizzically. "What is this thing, this duel?"

"It means we fight, you and I, with none other involved. We fight anywhere you want, either until one of us is injured, or to the death. The winner takes and keeps my woman. Only then will it be fair and honorable. You may decide where we fight. You may choose if we fight till injured, or to the death. I will decide what weapons are to be used."

The Indian considered, then nodded his head. "It is good. All will be final, honorable." He swung around to his men, gave them a few sharp commands and returned his attention to Johnny.

"We fight at my village. To the death. My people will be made to understand. If you win, you and the woman may leave in freedom. Should I win, the marriage ritual will take place at once."

He jabbed his mount with his heels, and it reared up dramatically. "Onto your horse, Stew-ert. It is a handsome beast. I shall be glad to add it and the mare to my string when I have won."

Johnny mounted the stallion with new hope. He had bought a little time. Now he must think hard and well about the proper weapon to use against the Pawnee chief. He knew he was at a disadvantage. He was not a man born to action. Neither had he any special martial skills to call to his aid. He did, however, have love and right on his side. Surely God would help him, for Maggie must be at least as precious to Him. And hadn't David vanquished Goliath under equally impossible odds?

In a haze of dust from the Indian ponies ahead of him, Johnny followed the braves back to their village, back to his woman.

Maggie woke, confused, in a dim, smoky cave. She opened her eyes wider and tried to take in her surroundings. She was lying on something soft and smoothly furry, with the smell of peat and smoke about it. It was a rich, strong aroma—a surprisingly comforting one.

There was a scrape of pots next to her, and she turned her head slightly to look into the face of an Indian woman. The nightmare returned. All of it— her foolish late walk to the spring, her capture by Red Eagle, his wife Corn Girl.

Maggie tried to sit, but a strong dizziness overcame her and she sank back into the buffalo robes. Corn Girl reached for a dampened scrap of buckskin and wiped Maggie's face. She spoke slowly, comfortingly. Maggie wished she could understand the words. The woman moved away for a moment to return with something steaming in a bowl. She motioned for Maggie to try to sit up again, to taste from the bowl.

Maggie struggled to acquiesce and finally was upright, a little less dizzy this time. She tasted from the bowl held out to her and gagged. The brew was hot and bitter. Poison? She studied the other woman's eyes. No. There was only concern written there. It must be an herbal remedy of the Indian's concoction, something with which she was unfamiliar.

Another sip was taken, and strength began returning to her limbs. Maggie held the bowl close to her lips with two trembling hands. She drank everything left and dropped again into her soft mattress. Corn Girl smiled. She carefully placed the bowl away to sketch out evocative motions. Maggie was to rest. She, Corn Girl, must return to the fields. Maggie nodded understanding and drifted off to sleep as Red Eagle's eldest wife quietly disappeared.

Maggie dozed fitfully, her dreams pierced with sharp, nightmarish visions. There was her baby, growing thin and wan, unable even to cry. Jamie— also rail thin—was riding a painted pony, feverishly trying to shoot an arrow at a huge, monolithic beast thundering down upon him. Maggie twisted and turned, trying to escape the images. New ones appeared. Now it was Johnny. He was entwined in the viselike grip of an enemy. The enemy's arms were thick and sinuous, like some vast prehistoric snake. Johnny was growing paler and paler. He was bleeding around his head and face. Maggie fought the dream, fought the terror. Suddenly she sat up like a shot, completely awake and aware. Completely lucid.

Someone had entered the lodge and was coming close to her. She tried to adjust her eyes to the dim light. It was not Corn Girl. Instinctively she knew it was not a woman at all. The movements were too stealthy. Had Red Eagle returned? No. He would not sneak into his own lodge. He would come as a conqueror, to take what he felt was rightly his.

Terror crept slowly, steadily up Maggie's spine. The feeling had reached her neck when the hated face of Snake appeared above hers, leering. Her eyes raced down his unwashed body to the hands reaching out for her. Maggie opened her mouth to scream.

The hunting party, with Johnny hard on its heels, arrived at the village in a cloud of dust and barking dogs. Johnny had only a moment to take in the huts and the expressions of surprise on the faces of the toothless old women sitting in the sun. Then he was off his horse, mad with the need to find his wife, to assure himself that she was alive and well.

He'd barely touched the ground when a piercing scream rang through the village. Johnny did not stop to think. He raced toward the sound, followed by Red Eagle, equally distressed.

The scream rang out again, and Johnny located its source. It came from the slightly larger lodge in the center of the settlement. He'd never heard Meg scream, but he knew definitively it was she. His hand reached for the only weapon he possessed— the hunting knife at his belt—as he ducked his tall frame to enter the hut.

The scream was coming from a pile of furs and bodies. Knife poised, Johnny drew back his arm to propel the blade into the alien back. He paused as the head was raised and two eyes black with hatred met his.

"Get up and fight like a man, or I'll stab you in the back like you deserve!"

Johnny's growled words were registered. Their meaning was clear in any language. Snake rose in one sinuous movement. When his right hand appeared it, too, was sporting a blade. Hunched beneath the low dome of the lodge's roof, the two men faced each other. Their frozen bodies turned mobile as a feinting dance of death began.

Snake's blade shot out first, grazing Johnny's neck. Johnny ignored the warm trickle of blood that began to ooze from the wound, ignored the hot glow from the dying embers of fire near his feet, ignored even the silent eyes of both Meg and Red Eagle, watching. He knew only one thing. This man, this man who had dared to touch his wife, to make her scream with such hopelessness—this man deserved to die.

Johnny did not know it, but he was screaming himself. He was yelling the war cry of his Highland ancestors, the cry of battle heard a hundred years past over the plains of Culloden. His mouth opened yet again, sending out another bloodcurdling shriek as he moved in on Snake, shoving aside the Indian's bloodied knife as if it were naught.

He thrust, and felt his own blade burrow into taut flesh. But it was a superficial wound. Stung, Snake shook him off as he would a mere wasp, and charged with fresh fury. Again and again, Johnny thrust and parried, summoning almost superhuman strength to dispatch this filth that would dare to violate his Maggie.

At last, with a bizarre twist of his body, Snake lunged at him, his eyes glazing in surprise as he felt himself impaled on Johnny's knife. Equally surprised, Johnny shoved him away and watched him fall in slow motion across the fire, crushing a pottery bowl beneath his weight.

Johnny stood staring until the acrid smell of burning flesh hit his nostrils. Only then did he realize that his enemy was dead. Snake had ended the matter himself, though it was Johnny's blade that had delivered the fatal blow.

Maggie was waiting, her eyes large with the horror of what they had witnessed. Her husband said nothing, but took her into his arms.

His voice returned slowly. "You are alive, my love. You are unharmed?"

"Oh, Johnny!" She clung closer. "Yes. Yes! Snake, he. . . . He didn't—"

Johnny ignored the implications of that left unsaid. "I've come to take you back home. The children will be missing you. And I have great need for you, too."

"Johnny. I was going to escape, tonight . . . but I felt so weak. They helped me . . . the women—" She paused, gasping for breath between the sobs that had started, unwanted. "They were very kind. And he—Red Eagle—he was, too, in his own way. . . . And then, and then, the Snake came—" She burst into another spasm of sobs.

"Hush. Save it for later. You're safe now. I have but one more thing to do."

Maggie choked, but her tears ebbed at the sudden

iron in her husband's voice. "What must you do?"

"I must buy your freedom. By killing Red Eagle."

"Need it come to that? Need there be more blood shed this day?"

"Yes. But it will be done honorably. A gentleman's duel—"

Suddenly, from his obscure position just inside the entrance, Red Eagle sprang into the center of a room, flashing a knife. Johnny had not planned to take him just yet. Not here. Not in front of Maggie, who had had enough of killing for one day.

But Red Eagle was bending over Snake. Wielding his blade skillfully, he took a fistful of the straight black hair. Methodically he carved off the hank and its skin. He stood up then, raising it high.

"You forget something, Stew-ert. This belongs to you."

Johnny waved aside the offer. "It is worthless to me. A snake may shed his skin many times, but it does not make of him a man."

Red Eagle nodded silent agreement, but still blocked the way. "Stew-ert—" he began again.

Johnny, feeling the knife still in his hand, wiped its blade along one pants leg, then held it up, a signal that he was ready for the next battle.

"Stew-ert, unknown, you have made me the gift of a great boon. This Snake that lies dead at our feet was my sworn enemy. He was but half Pawnee, the other half the gift of a wandering war party of Comanche. He strove for my power, my wives. He insulted the woman of my heart. Your wife. You have honored me by your action. For this, I will return your woman."

Johnny's fist tightened on the knife, not daring to believe what he was hearing. "You mean—"

"I believe still that I am stronger than you. I would have won her freely and with honor. But that will be left to the heavens. The Great Spirit guides us both. You may go."

Behind him, Johnny heard Meg's stifled sob of relief.

He turned once more to the chief. "You are a man of honor, indeed. A worthy foe, and a worthy friend. I wish that your tribe may thrive, and your women bear you many strong sons. And tonight, when I pray to my God, the Great Spirit, I will thank Him for Red Eagle, my brother."

Johnny passed out of the hut into the bright sunlight, Maggie beside him. They were free.

A Letter To Our Readers

Dear Reader:

In order that we might better contribute to your reading enjoyment, we would appreciate your taking a few minutes to respond to the following questions and return to:

Karen Carroll, Editor
Heartsong Presents
P.O. Box 719
Uhrichsville, Ohio 44683

1. Did you enjoy reading *Gone West*?
   - ❏ Very much. I would like to see more books by this author!
   - ❏ Moderately

   - ❏ I would have enjoyed it more if

   _____

2. Where did you purchase this book?_____

   _____

3. What influenced your decision to purchase this book?
❏ Cover	❏ Back cover copy
❏ Title	❏ Friends
❏ Publicity	❏ Other _____

4. Please rate the following elements from 1 (poor) to 10 (superior).
   - ❑ Heroine ❑ Plot
   - ❑ Hero ❑ Inspirational theme
   - ❑ Setting ❑ Secondary characters

5. What settings would you like to see in Heartsong Presents Books?

   _____

   _____

6. What are some inspirational themes you would like to see treated in future books?

   _____

   _____

7. Would you be interested in reading other Heartsong Presents Books?
   - ❑ Very interested
   - ❑ Moderately interested
   - ❑ Not interested

8. Please indicate your age range:
   - ❑ Under 18 ❑ 25-34 ❑ 46-55
   - ❑ 18-24 ❑ 35-45 ❑ Over 55

Name _____

Occupation _____

Address _____

City _____ State _____ Zip _____

HEARTS♥NG PRESENTS books are inspirational
romances in contemporary and historical settings, designed to
give you an enjoyable, spirit-lifting reading experience.

HEARTSONG PRESENTS TITLES AVAILABLE NOW:

HAVE YOU MISSED ANY OF THESE TITLES?

These additional titles in our Romance Reader series contain two complete romance novels for the price of one. You'll enjoy hours of great inspirational reading. Published at $7.95 each, these titles are available through Heartsong Presents for $3.97 each.

Great New Inspirational Fiction
from HEART♥NG PRESENTS

Biblical Novel Collection #1
by Lee Webber
Two complete inspirational novels in one volume.

_____ BNC1 **CALL ME SARAH**—Can Sarah, like Queen Esther
be used by God . . . even as a slave in Herod's place?
CAPERNAUM CENTURION—One Centurion's
life is irrevocably changed by his encounter with a
certain Nazarene.

CITRUS COUNTY MYSTERY COLLECTION № 1
by Mary Carpenter Reid
Two complete inspirational mystery novels in one volume.

_____ CCM1 **TOPATOPA**—Can Alyson Kendricks make an history
village come alive . . . without becoming history herself?
DRESSED FOR DANGER—Roxanne Shelton's
fashion designs were the key to her success . . . but
did they unlock a closet of secrets?

_BOTH COLLECTIONS ARE AVAILABLE FOR $3.97 EACH THROUGH
HEARTSONG PRESENTS. ORIGINALLY PUBLISHED AT $7.95 EACH._

LOVE A GREAT LOVE STORY?

Introducing Heartsong Presents —
Your Inspirational Book Club

Heartsong Presents Christian romance reader's service will provide you with four never before published romance titles every month! In fact, your books will be mailed to you at the same time advance copies are sent to book reviewers. You'll preview each of these new and unabridged books before they are released to the general public.

These books are filled with the kind of stories you have been longing for—stories of courtship, chivalry, honor, and virtue. Strong characters and riveting plot lines will make you want to read on and on. Romance is not dead, and each of these romantic tales will remind you that Christian faith is still the vital ingredient in an intimate relationship filled with true love and honest devotion.

Sign up today to receive your first set. Send no money now. We'll bill you only $9.97 post-paid with your shipment. Then every month you'll automatically receive the latest four "hot off the press" titles for the same low post-paid price of $9.97. That's a savings of 50% off the $4.95 cover price. When you consider the exaggerated shipping charges of other book clubs, your savings are even greater!

THERE IS NO RISK—you may cancel at any time without obligation. And if you aren't completely satisfied with any selection, return it for an immediate refund.

TO JOIN, just complete the coupon below, mail it today, and get ready for hours of wholesome entertainment.

Now you can curl up, relax, and enjoy some great reading full of the warmhearted spirit of romance.

— — — Curl up with Heartsong! — — —

YES! Sign me up for Heartsong!

NEW MEMBERSHIPS WILL BE SHIPPED IMMEDIATELY!
Send no money now. We'll bill you only $9.97 post-paid with your first shipment of four books. Or for faster action, call toll free 1-800-847-8270.

NAME _____

ADDRESS _____

CITY _____ STATE / ZIP _____
  MAIL TO: HEARTSONG / P.O. Box 719 Uhrichsville, Ohio 44683
YES II